"I said *if* I wanted you..."

His eyes were hard as they moved up and down her body. "I can assure you I don't."

Her cheeks tingled as if she'd been slapped. "So what *are* you doing here? My grandmother paid a pretty penny to get you out—more pennies than she could afford, as it turned out."

Bracing one foot on the car fender, he began pulling suitcases out of the trunk. "Things do look a little...neglected. Tell me, who does your lawns now, Amanda? Some new man who attends to your—" he snapped the trunk shut and looked at her insolently "—your needs?"

Shocked by the frontal attack, she said the first hurtful thing that occurred to her. "Oh, dear, I hope you're not applying again," she said in mock concern. "It's not that your work wasn't adequate. We just found your prices a bit...exorbitant."

KATHLEEN O'BRIEN, an American author from sunny Florida, started out as a newspaper feature writer and television critic, but happily traded that job in for marriage to an upwardly mobile journalist, motherhood and the opportunity to work on a novel. She finds romance writing especially satisfying, as it allows her to look for—and find—all the good things in life. Readers will find this author's work fresh, warm and exciting—brimming with romance.

Books by Kathleen O'Brien

HARLEQUIN PRESENTS
1011—SUNSWEPT SUMMER

Don't miss any of our special offers. Write to us at the following address for information on our newest releases.

Harlequin Reader Service
901 Fuhrmann Blvd., P.O. Box 1397, Buffalo, NY 14240
Canadian address: P.O. Box 603,
Fort Erie, Ont. L2A 5X3

KATHLEEN O'BRIEN

white midnight

Harlequin Books

TORONTO • NEW YORK • LONDON
AMSTERDAM • PARIS • SYDNEY • HAMBURG
STOCKHOLM • ATHENS • TOKYO • MILAN

Harlequin Presents first edition July 1989
ISBN 0-373-11189-4

CHAPTER ONE

HALFWAY DOWN THE HILL Amanda knew she wouldn't be able to catch him. Her legs, clumsy from exhaustion, still churned beneath her, but the lights of his car were speeding smoothly away, as though he couldn't wait to be rid of Mount Larkin and the whole Larkin family, her especially.

But she couldn't give up, though her throat was too dry to swallow, and the August wind whipped the tears off her cheeks before they could reach her lips. She stumbled over a glinting silver rock, caught herself on a pine branch and kept on.

"Drake!" she cried, but she knew he couldn't hear her. His battered little car needed, among other things, a new muffler.... How they had laughed at that just yesterday. She, who was chauffeured in a Cadillac, had fallen in love in a beat-up Volkswagen. "Drake, wait!"

But he was too far away. She heard an owl answer, but she couldn't hear the roar of the faulty muffler. Too far. The headlights had already turned off of Larkin Road, onto the highway that would take him away forever.

"No, Olivia," she whispered fiercely, though she knew, without even looking back, that her grandmother was still up at the house, silhouetted in the bright carriage lights of Mount Larkin's Georgian entryway, frozen by her fury at Amanda's defiance. "No, Olivia. No!"

There was only one hope of stopping Drake, one shortcut. She twisted away from the path, hurtling herself down the steep, uncivilized edge of the property. The wet Georgia clay slid under her bare feet, and the kudzu vines grabbed her ankles. She lost sight of the headlights for one panicked instant as her balance tilted. She skidded a few yards on one leg and then righted herself, and found the spots of white that sped along like two stars that had fallen from the sky.

Suddenly the ground sheered off sharply, and the downhill momentum took over, flinging her faster than her tired legs could have managed on their own. Her heart throbbed in her ears as though looking for a way out of her body, and her lungs struggled audibly for air. But the lights were closer now.

Too close! she thought wildly.

Just a millisecond before the car hit her, thought started again. It was strange thought—a subconscious assimilation of color and shape. The wrong color and shape. The wrong car. Not Drake, after all. Drake Daniels still roared through the night, her grandmother's check for ten thousand dollars on the seat beside him, where she, Amanda, should have been. She heard herself cry out as the pain began and the world caught fire around her....

"No!"

Wrenching herself awake, Amanda bolted upright in bed and stared at the moonlit room. Oh, god, not again. Biting her lower lip so that no more sounds could escape, she pulled her damp auburn hair back from her forehead and listened. Had she awakened her aunt? At first there was only the painful thud of her heart, but then she heard a soft swishing from the next room. Cicely would be slipping into her quilted housecoat. Amanda groaned lightly, dropping her head to her hand as she waited for the inevitable anxious whisper.

It came quickly. "Mandy?" As usual, her aunt stood diffidently in the doorway between their rooms to give Amanda privacy in which to collect herself. "Are you all right, honey?"

Oh, that cursed dream! Now Cicely would start worrying again, and there was no reason to. The nightmare was six years old. It was meaningless, really, just an old, faded videotape her dreams played in error every now and then, as though the computer of her subconscious had a bad wire somewhere. But try convincing Cicely of that!

Releasing her stinging lip and dragging a deep breath into her clenched lungs, Amanda pushed the heavy covers back and swung her legs onto the floor. "I'm fine, Cicely, really." She forced a smile into her voice. "Why don't you try to go back to sleep?"

But as though Amanda's voice had been the signal to come in, Cicely traversed the room, her soft pink mules silent on the thick carpet, and perched on the edge of the bed like a small pink bird. "You had another one of those dreams, didn't you?"

"I don't remember," Amanda lied somewhat crossly, then stood, avoiding her aunt's consoling hand. She knew Cicely meant well, but a person's dreams, at least, should be private. Light from the cloudy moon pooled in front of the bedroom windows and, for want of a better destination, she headed toward it. She walked slowly—her right leg was always a little stiffer when she first woke up. Later, when she had done her exercises, the limp would be almost unnoticeable. It had taken six years, but she had recovered, physically as well as emotionally, better than anyone had thought she would. Only sleep could make it seem important—Drake Daniels, the accident, or the slight lameness they had left behind.

Ignoring her aunt's hurt silence, Amanda stared down at the west patio, where a shining carpet of leaves promised another typical Georgia wintery morning, cold and miserably wet. The sight disappointed her. She had hoped to paint today, but her style wasn't well suited to the silvers and browns of winter. She needed brighter colors—yellow sun and blue sky....

It would be clear and sunny in Florida now, all cotton-ball clouds floating over periwinkle lakes. She'd like to paint Julie under that Florida sky.... Suddenly she missed her daughter terribly. So often, after these nightmares, she had tiptoed into Julie's room for comfort. And she had found it, in the artless tumble of golden hair around the little girl's face, in the small, half-opened fist that sank into the white eyelet quilt. She had steadied her own breathing by matching it to Julie's, and usually Julie gleefully discovered her there in the morning, asleep on the old rocker. "That's not a bed, Mommy," Julie would laugh. "It's not?" Amanda would answer, teasingly astonished. And the day would begin, untainted by the night.

But she mustn't begrudge Julie her special trip, her vacation under the blue Florida skies. She'd be back in a couple of weeks, in time for Christmas. Maybe by then this sopping rain would have turned to snow. Julie loved the snow.

And besides, Amanda didn't really have time for painting today, anyhow, not with the new guest arriving.

"What time is it?" Amanda could have turned around and checked the china mantel clock herself, but she already regretted her curt tone and wanted to let her aunt know she wasn't angry.

"It's only five o'clock," Cicely said, stifling a yawn. "Amanda—"

"These curtains need cleaning," Amanda interrupted, knowing her aunt had been about to discuss the dream again. But housekeeping was Cicely's first love, and she rose instantly to the bait.

"Do they?" she asked quickly. "We'd better put it on our list. You know that fine Irish lace will just fall apart if you don't keep it clean."

Amanda nodded absently, running her fingers down the soft curtains that were pulled halfway across the wide tall window. Moonlight backlit the gauzy fabric, and her artistic eye appreciated its creamy glow even while her more pragmatic side considered the cleaning issue.

"Yes, well, we'd better put it at the bottom of the list," she suggested dryly. "The paying guests never see our rooms. We'd better fix *their* curtains first, when we can fix anything at all."

She let go of the lace with a wry grin. If she simply *had* to have nightmares, she asked herself, why dream about Drake Daniels? Why didn't she dream about something more immediate—like tomorrow's visit to the bank? Now there was something to haunt your sleep! She pictured with distaste Mr. Tindal's neat hands, nails square and immaculate, folded on his big oak desk, and his neat face, with eyes as cold as the gold pin on his tie, explaining the details of the new contract, the requirements of the new investor.

She shook herself mentally. She shouldn't complain. She should be glad there *was* an investor. They were hardly waiting in line to invest in Mount Larkin. Slowly—too slowly to suit most money men—Mount Larkin was making a name for itself, especially among literary and artistic circles. Its quaint Southern charm appealed to artists of all kinds, and gradually the word was spreading. Maybe if this new guest, this Roger Stowe whose murder mysteries were becoming so popular, liked Mount Larkin, too, it would help.

But none of that was likely to impress Mr. Tindal and the executive from the Vermont Innkeeping Investment Corp. tomorrow. She remembered a line or two Mr. Tindal had let drop on earlier visits about the unreliable nature of artists. The banker and the investor might well want to change Mount Larkin's character altogether. Oh, she hoped this investor was a decent person, a fair person, not too intrusive.

Anxiety pinched at her again, and she turned away from the window. She looked at her aunt's slight form with a sudden rush of love. They'd been through a lot together, the three Larkin women—the wispy maiden aunt, the young widow and the laughing Julie—and they would make it through these financial troubles, too. They were an unconventional family, to say the least, but they were happier than they had ever been in the old days, when Olivia Larkin had ruled Mount Larkin with an iron fist. An iron heart, too, Amanda sometimes thought.

But Olivia was gone, the much overrated Larkin fortune was gone, and so was Drake Daniels—except for the wretched dream. Amanda flipped on the overhead light and smiled at her aunt.

"Well, brooding won't get anything done, will it?" She held out her hand to help her aunt up from the bed. "It's my day to fix breakfast, and I think I'll go down early to make Webster some muffins. He'll be up soon for his morning run."

Cicely smiled, too, and shook her head ruefully. "Webster really shouldn't run in this weather, at his age. It's too cold and too damp."

"He's only a few years older than you," Amanda reproved. "That's hardly ancient. And besides, it's running that keeps him so trim and handsome. You know you wouldn't have him any other way."

She grinned as she caught her aunt's blush out of the corner of her eye. It was wonderful to see Cicely so happy. Webster Bronson, a retired business executive, stayed at Mount Larkin whenever he was in Atlanta, and each visit was a little longer than the last.

This time, Amanda suspected, he might not leave at all. Just yesterday she had caught him furtively wrapping a small square box in silver Christmas paper. Amanda hadn't said a word but had simply given him a smile and a thumbs-up before heading back to the kitchen. It was high time Mount Larkin hosted a happy romance for a change.

As soon as she started her shower running, Amanda remembered one last instruction and stuck her head out of the bathroom door. "Oh, Cicely—I've decided to put Roger Stowe in my old room. Can you stock the mini bar and make sure there are enough towels in the bath?"

Her aunt looked surprised. "Your old room? I thought we had decided on the blue room."

"I changed my mind. Roger Stowe may be our most important guest ever, and you know my room is the best one left, even if the curtains do need cleaning. We've got to make a good impression."

A good impression *was* important, she repeated to her reflection later—but was she maybe overdoing it a little? After all, Roger Stowe would judge Mount Larkin Bed and Breakfast by its comforts and its food, not the appearance of its owners. So why was she taking such unusual care with her makeup? She wrinkled her short nose at herself as she rolled on lipstick, regretting not for the first time in her life that she was five foot four, olive-eyed and only marginally auburn-haired, instead of a willowy titian beauty like the heroine of Roger Stowe's books.

She surveyed her wardrobe carefully for an outfit that would help. The budget hadn't allowed many shopping sprees lately, so the best she could find was a daffodil-colored skirt to wear under last year's forest-green sweater. Hardly high fashion, but yellow was a good color for her—it emphasized the auburn highlights in her hair, though it still fell lamentably short of titian. For good measure she tied a yellow ribbon around her glossy ponytail and stood back to survey the results.

Not exactly heroine material, but maybe Roger Stowe wouldn't be too disappointed. Silly, of course, to go to all this trouble for a man she'd never seen—but what was the harm in being silly? She couldn't go around forever being worried and disappointed, could she? That wouldn't get Mr. Tindal his money any faster. And besides, Julie would approve. Amanda winked at herself and turned around, her long thick ponytail bouncing as she took the wide stairs two at a time.

Half an hour later the muffins were just beginning to scent the air when Webster Bronson poked his head through the doorway. His gray eyes sparkled at the sight of the brightly lit kitchen, and he sniffed the air like an enthusiastic Spaniel.

"Oh, be still my heart! Can it be true? Muffins?" At Amanda's encouraging nod he came in, pulling the door shut on the dim, drizzling garden beyond. He plopped onto one of the wooden chairs and smiled at her.

"Marvelous Amanda. How *do* you Larkin women manage to look so gorgeous in the morning?" He ran his hand through his hair sadly, obviously aware that its dark wetness was not as becoming as its usual buoyant silver curls, and flicked a raindrop from his thick gray eyebrows.

Amanda laughed and patted his shoulder as she passed him on her way to the refrigerator. "It's my secret health plan," she said in a stage whisper. "I made a solemn vow years ago never, ever to go jogging."

Webster slapped his waterlogged sweat suit and sighed. "Beautiful *and* brilliant! You're going to make someone a wonderful wife, Amanda. It's not many women who can be up at six-thirty, with makeup on their lovely faces and blueberry muffins perfuming the air around them.''

She tossed him a kitchen towel to dry his hair and brought him a short glass of orange juice. "Is that all you want from a wife, Webster?'' she teased, sitting down on the edge of the table beside him. "Lipstick and muffins and insomnia?''

"It's a start.'' He tossed back the juice like a neat whiskey. "Of course, it would help if she liked to dance and sing and hang out with old codgers like me.''

Amanda smiled, picturing Cicely, who right about now was probably singing something from *Oklahoma* as she tidied her room. "Hmm... I'll give it some serious thought and see if I might know anyone like that.''

He answered her smile with a raffish grin. "Do that. You might even ask your aunt how she feels about dancing.'' He tilted his chair onto its back legs and squinted at Amanda. "So, what are you looking for in a husband? I have a nephew who likes muffins....''

Amanda pretended to consider, swinging her long legs that dangled from the dark oak table and nibbling on a fingernail. "Let's see. Devastatingly attractive, of course. Smart. And a quick wit—sense of humor is awfully important, don't you think? Exciting hobbies, a marvelous career, sophisticated, glamorous....''

She slipped off the table and smoothed her skirt in exaggerated resignation. "But Paul Newman's already married. I guess I'll just have to stay single."

Just in time to hear Amanda's last sentence Cicely appeared in the doorway, and Webster's eyes lit up at the sight of her. "Cicely! Not a moment too soon! I'm just trying to convince Amanda that it's a crime for the Larkin ladies to remain single. Help me!"

Cicely's soft gray eyes darted toward Amanda. Her forehead creased anxiously. "Amanda is a widow, Webster. She doesn't want to get married again."

"Sure she does," he retorted, undaunted. "Look at that pretty girl. Does she look like she's ready to settle back and be a widow and a mommy for the rest of her life?" He grinned at Amanda, who wrinkled her nose back at him. "Naw, Doc Hamilton's been dead for three years now. That's long enough. That's not the problem. Problem is her standards are too high. You should have heard her describing the only man she'd ever marry—a blue-eyed heartthrob, nothing less."

Cicely's eyes widened to shocked circles, and her ladylike pink lips formed a silent O as she faced Amanda.

Realizing what her aunt must be thinking, Amanda hastened to explain. "Paul Newman. I was talking about Paul Newman."

The nervous color receded from her aunt's cheeks, and she smiled feebly. "Of course. Well, of course." She began pulling silver out of the chest rapidly, preparing to set the table. "Well, he's a very handsome man, no doubt about that. And quite devoted to his wife, they say. A little old for you, though..."

Amanda groaned inwardly and tried to tune out the older woman's anxious chatter. She gathered up the place settings and walked along in front of her aunt, laying down the creamy woven mats and folding lemon-yellow napkins around the long table. Poor Cicely. Sometimes it seemed she had suffered as much from the episode with Drake Daniels as Amanda herself. It had been terribly hard at first, of course, but with six years' practice, Amanda had learned how to block out conscious thoughts of Drake. Sometimes, though, when the early-evening sky was that peculiar cobalt blue or when the scent of honeysuckle rushed around a corner, catching her unaware... But she certainly didn't, like Cicely, go all flustered and fluttery simply at the mention of blue eyes.

"Oh, I think we'd better set an extra place this morning," she said, turning suddenly and nearly running into her aunt. "I don't know what time Roger Stowe is arriving, but we don't want him to feel unwelcome."

"No one has ever felt unwelcome at Mount Larkin," Webster put in gallantly, pressing Cicely's hand as she put down his gleaming silver spoon.

Watching the gratified blush spread across her aunt's pale cheeks, Amanda suppressed the response that sprang to her lips, turning instead to fill the pewter pitcher with rich fresh cream. No one? Well, Webster couldn't know that there had been a day, long ago, when she had been made to feel quite unwelcome indeed. Back before it was an inn, when the Larkins were rich, or at least wanted the world to think they were, old Olivia Larkin had hardly cheered the arrival of her little orphaned granddaughter. But she had, in her way, accepted her, had made her a proud Larkin possession. And therefore the upstart Drake Daniels had not been welcomed, either, except through the service entrance.

But she was getting as foolish as Cicely, letting the most casual word conjure up ghosts. She had paid enough for the mistakes of those days. The accounts were closed. Perhaps she couldn't control her subconscious mind, which seemed determined to relive that last mad race for happiness in her dreams, but she certainly could, and would, control her conscious thoughts. She buried the memory of Drake Daniels a little deeper and turned to greet the rest of her guests, who were already arriving for their breakfast.

"Good morning, Lina, Tom." She waved them toward the table, where Cicely had been filling glasses. "Start with juice and coffee, won't you? The eggs will be ready in a jiffy."

As the guests exchanged greetings and seated themselves, she whipped out her frying pan and began melting butter, annoyed with herself for running late. Some way to build a reputation! She stirred the butter fiercely. She couldn't afford to let her standards slip, not now that the new investor would be looking over their shoulders.

She listened to the others as she shook spices into the eggs. Tom Wyndham was typically chatty as he launched into his daily update on the progress of his painting. He had been up for hours, he told them proudly, because the raindrops falling from the pine needles had been too beautiful to miss. Amanda smiled. Tom was thirty-five, but his talent kept him as enthusiastic as a teen. Inspiration would jolt through

his dreams, and he would clamber out of bed to catch
it on his canvas. He was a real artist, and it would take
more than a drizzly winter morning to dampen his
spirits. It was really quite flattering that he admired
Amanda's simple watercolors. In fact, he had even
taken some of them to a gallery owner he knew, and
if the owner liked them... But that was a long shot,
and Amanda wouldn't allow herself to count on it.

Carolina Travers was just the opposite. It was
something of a surprise to see her at the breakfast table at all. She was the daughter of one of Cicely's
friends, and had been given her two-week visit to
Mount Larkin as a college-graduation present. Ordi-
narily she stayed up half the night writing poetry and
then wandered lazily out of her room around noon.

And to what, Amanda wondered, did they owe the
pleasure of Lina's company this morning? She glanced
at her curiously as she took the ham out of the refrigerator. Ahh... Lina was wearing her loveliest dress,
and her golden locks tumbled fetchingly around a
bright blue ribbon. Amanda understood instinctively
that Lina, too, was ready to meet their exciting new
guest.

Blushing as she thought of her own beribboned
ponytail, Amanda carried the eggs to the table self-
consciously. Even Cicely, she observed, had added a
lace collar to her plain sweater. Good grief! They were
as bad as three broody hens.

Tom Wyndham noticed it, too, now that all three
ladies were seated together at the table. He looked
from one to the other, then turned to Webster and
grinned. "Is it my imagination, Webster, or are the
ladies looking like something straight off a Sargent

canvas this morning? It isn't someone's birthday, is it?''

Lina laughed, a musical tinkle, and shook her curls. ''Oh, Tom, of course not. We're just excited because Roger Stowe is coming today, aren't we, Amanda?''

Amanda smiled sheepishly, amazed once again at Lina's complete lack of inhibition, but Webster broke in before she could answer. ''Why? What's so special about this Roger Stowe? You've never even seen him, have you? I hear he's publicity shy.''

''You've never seen Shakespeare, either, and you'd be pretty excited if he came to stay, wouldn't you?'' Carolina's logic might have been a little thin, but her reverent tone left no doubt about her feelings for Roger Stowe.

''Shakespeare!'' Webster almost choked on his coffee and clanked the cup into its saucer incredulously. ''Shakespeare! Why, this Stowe fellow has only written two books—detective novels at that! What does he have to do with Shakespeare?''

Lina just raised her lovely eyebrows, but Cicely surprised Amanda by jumping in to defend Stowe gently. ''They are such wonderful books, though, Webster. His detective is a fascinating character, and his plots are marvelous. You should read them. Really you should. Even the *New York Times* said you should.''

''Yeah, I saw that article,'' Tom agreed. ''I told myself I'd have to read the books, but I've just never had the time. I hope he won't be offended.'' He filled his mouth with eggs and concluded with a sigh, ''Perhaps he understands, being creative himself. Art is such a stern mistress!''

The women laughed at the image of the sunny Tom as a driven genius, but Webster's face was still sour, and Amanda smiled into her teacup. All his blustering did not hide the fact that he was jealous—jealous of her aunt's interest in the mysterious author who was coming to stay at Mount Larkin. She glanced over at her aunt, wondering if she was aware of it.

But Cicely's face just wore its usual worried look as she listened to Webster's grumbling. "Besides," he was continuing, "even if the guy wrote *War and Peace*, why all the ribbons and lace?" He stabbed at his eggs. "Looks to me like you're expecting some kind of movie star, when for all you know he might be just an ornery old codger like me. Or worse."

"Oh, no, not Roger Stowe," Lina said dreamily, her blue eyes glistening, apparently unaware that there was anything thoughtless in her words. "He's young, and he's handsome, and he knows more about romance than any man I've ever met."

Webster tsked loudly. "You don't know that. You've never laid eyes on the man."

But Lina was impervious, lost in her fantasy. "Oh, yes, I do. I can tell by his books. His detective is so handsome, so much in love with the heroine." She sighed heavily. "Even though he knows he can't have her. He doesn't even know her name. It's tragic. It's beautiful."

Much to her chagrin, even Amanda felt a curious ache in the pit of her stomach as she thought about the novels, which she had read only recently. Though Lina made them sound rather silly, more like comic books, basically she was right. Roger Stowe's novels were, for all their cold-blooded, murderous plots, the most sensuous and romantic books she had ever read. She, too, found it hard to believe that such passionate love stories came from any "ornery old codger."

But Webster just gave a grunt of disgust. "Sounds soppy to me," he told his plate.

"He *is* good, isn't he?" Amanda agreed finally, when Lina's sighing silence had gone on so long that the two men were exchanging looks. "It'll be interesting to see what he's like."

"He's a creep," Webster insisted stubbornly. "If he weren't, he wouldn't be such a recluse. He's probably the exact opposite of his hero. His publishers probably won't let him show himself for fear he'll kill sales. He's probably fifty if he's a day. He's probably as bald as a billiard ball. He's probably a ninety-eight pound weakling. He's probably—"

"Think again," Lina interrupted hastily. Amanda hadn't heard the sound of a car, but Lina, who faced the kitchen door, obviously saw something she liked. She was sitting on the edge of her chair, her eyes as brightly blue as her hair ribbon. "He just got here. He parked back here, and he's walking around to the front door now. He *is* wonderful! He's even better than I thought."

Trying to ignore the slight acceleration of her heart Lina's words caused, Amanda excused herself and pushed back her heavy chair. She forced herself to walk slowly, and the doorbell sounded its deep tones twice before she reached the front foyer. The others had followed close behind her, and were even now whispering in a cluster at the edge of the hall.

Lina's piercing whisper could be heard distinctly. "See?" she hissed triumphantly. "He's perfect. He looks just like his detective. I told you!"

Amanda froze, her hand locked around the brass doorknob, unable to turn. Roger Stowe stood patiently outside the door, his long trim body framed in the sidelights just where the awestruck group indoors could see him perfectly. His faded blue jeans hugged his muscular legs, and the collar of his glistening windbreaker was turned up against the rain. His thick fair hair was darkened by the moisture, and one glossy lock curled around the collar.

Amanda's thoughts slid helplessly out of her mind, like water from an overturned glass, as she met the deep cobalt-blue eyes through the window. Lina was right. He looked wonderful. He looked perfect.

He looked just like Drake Daniels.

CHAPTER TWO

"AMANDA! Open the door!"

Amanda heard Lina's words dimly, as though they were on the wrong side of a thick shield that surrounded her. Even the younger woman's light laughter bounced off the shield without breaking through, as she added, "I know he's a knockout, but you don't have to go into an absolute trance. Let the man in before he gets soaked."

Lina nudged her, but Amanda could barely feel the touch, her body caught in its own frantic turmoil. Her breath came shallow and rapid, and her heart seemed to beat high up in her throat. Perspiration tickled at her hairline, but her lips were dry. She felt as if she'd been running. And in a way, she realized numbly, still staring at the tall man outside the window, she had been. For six long years she had been running from the ghost of Drake Daniels, from the echoes of his easy laughter and the burning memory of his strong arms.

But, like in a nightmare, all her running had taken her nowhere. Here she was, back where she started, once again staring into the deep blue eyes of the only man she had ever loved, and feeling herself falling....

Falling, and laughing. Onto a sun-warmed pile of grass clippings at the far edge of the Larkin property.

Drake's hard arms were catching her, wrapping her close against his naked gleaming torso and pulling her to the ground.

"No fair!" Still laughing breathlessly, she tossed a handful of grass like green confetti into his golden hair. "You're in better shape than I am."

His blue eyes burned as they swept across her face and down to where her yellow sundress was rising and falling with her labored breathing. "I'm sorry, ma'am," he said, his Texas drawl exaggerated, as though to hide the slight thickness in his voice. "I'm going to have to disagree with that."

She tried to laugh, but her breath stalled somewhere in her throat, and the sound that came out was more like a small gasp. The cotton sundress was tight and heavy across her suddenly sensitive breasts, and the unfamiliar sensation thrilled her.

"Drake," she whispered, "kiss me."

His arms tensed around her. "I'd better not, Mandy."

"Please." Resting her head against his chest, she ran her hands down his back. He had been working hard, sculpting hedges along the west border of her grandmother's garden all afternoon, and sweat had oiled the rippling muscles to slippery hot columns. They tightened as her hands slithered up and down, and she was lost in the intoxicating touch. The wet gold mats of hair on his broad chest dampened her sundress as she pressed closer, and she felt her nipples hardening against the fabric.

He must have felt it, too, for he pulled away suddenly, his warm wet skin slipping easily out of her grasp.

"Stop it, Mandy," he growled, running his hands through his fair hair raggedly. "This isn't a game."

She lay back, still drugged by the feel and smell of him, hard and earthy in a way she had never known a man could be. Reaching over, she trailed her pink-tipped fingers slowly across his chest. "Don't you want to kiss me?" she asked, smiling hazily.

His answer was a curse, and the violence of it took her breath away. In one hard movement he straddled her, pushing her against the sweet grass, and grabbed her shoulders.

"Stop it, dammit!" His voice was strange, with a rusty quality she'd never heard before. "Don't play sorority games with me, Mandy. I'm not one of your idiotic college boys who'll chase around after your pretty virginal body like a kitten after a ball of yarn. I'm a man. Don't you know that yet?"

She didn't answer. She didn't even breathe. Of course she knew. She had always known. But never as much as now. He seemed huge suddenly, with his ribbons of golden muscle rigid and his face so close. She could feel the tension in his thighs as he fought to rein in both his anger and his passion.

"Do I want to kiss you?" His eyes locked on her lips and she felt them tingle. "You know damn well I do. But I can't stop there anymore, Mandy. I need more. I need all of you."

He tightened his grip on her shoulders and the complacency that had surrounded her earlier broke open like a dam. She began to tremble.

Suddenly she knew, as from a stroke of summer lightning, that he had, in the past weeks, become as necessary to her as the sun that shone above them now.

"Oh, Drake." She faltered under his hot waiting appraisal. She wanted to tell him he was right. She *was* young and sheltered and foolish. She was lucky he had waited this long, waited while fear held her back, while her grandmother's admonitions echoed through her frivolous head. "Remember, men won't buy what they can get for free, Amanda." How absurd such platitudes sounded out here, where love and need had come together in such a cataclysmic explosion.

But she didn't know how to put her feelings into words. The trembling increased, and she held shaking hands up toward his face. "Kiss me, Drake," she said again. "All of me."

For a long moment he stared, disbelieving, his breath coming hard from his full lips. His eyes raked her face, as though trying to see past the surface and into her soul. Finally, with a groan of surrender, he let his arms wrap around her back and arced her shaking body up to meet the hard need of his own.

It shouldn't have been so wonderful. The new-mown grass was sticky under her back...the sun poured mercilessly onto her upturned face. She was only nineteen, as naive and as virginal as he had suspected. He was tired from his day's labor.

And yet as soon as his hands and mouth began their urgent probing, a miraculous spiral of ecstasy began spinning deep within her. She knew no fear, no shame, there in the far corner of her grandmother's land, with only the ancient pines to shield her. Her abandoned cries of pleasure reverberated in the stillness, as strange and wonderful to her ears as the call of an exotic bird.

And when he at last drove into her, pain burst like a red sun and then was swept away forever on the whirling wind of passion.

Yes. He was a man. The only man she would ever love. And now she knew, as she cradled his drowsy head on her chest, dropping both tears and kisses onto the damp fair hair, she was a woman....

"Good heavens, Amanda, let me do it," her aunt's voice broke in, and Amanda caught an image of someone moving quickly forward to reach for the door.

Wrenched from her memories, Amanda dropped back instinctively, unable to speak the words that would warn her aunt. The click of the lock as Cicely twisted the knob was as sharp as the discharge of a pistol, and Amanda shivered in the rush of cold wet air as the big door swung wide.

She heard her aunt gasp as Drake Daniels stepped into the foyer. "Oh!" she breathed in a horrified undertone that she meant only Amanda to hear, clutching at her niece's cold hand. "Oh, dear!"

But Drake Daniels heard it, and a mirthless smile tugged one corner of his wide mouth. "Hi, there," he said, his deep Texas drawl achingly familiar.

His voice—his wonderful voice. It was true, then. She wasn't hallucinating. Drake Daniels was standing in her foyer. But why? Pieces of thoughts clattered through her brain like odd coins tossed on a table.

But everyone was waiting for her to say something, and she had to make some sense of this. He wasn't helping her at all. Damn his arrogance, standing there grinning at her consternation. What was he doing here?

Amanda dug her nails into the palms of her hands, trying to steady their shaking. The last time she had been with Drake Daniels, the last August night of their short hot summer, he had been exhausted from early-morning college courses, blistering afternoons land-scaping and long hours into the night working on his play. And yet she had been the one to fall asleep that night on the scratchy couch in his tiny apartment, soothed by the sound of the rain on the windows and the steady clatter of his typewriter. She remembered awakening slowly to the building heat of his lips on hers....

Confused, she tried to sort it out. Could he have gone from impoverished playwright to best-selling novelist in the past six years? Anger came to her res-cue, like water tossed on a fire, and her mind cleared. Of course he could have. The ten thousand dollars he had extorted from her grandmother could have bought a lot of typing paper.

Well, whoever he was and whatever his reasons for coming to Mount Larkin, he wasn't going to have the pleasure of rattling her composure. She wasn't any longer a naive nineteen-year-old whose heart was bursting with love and whose body was yearning for his touch. This time the scales were more evenly bal-anced. She was six years older—and eons wiser. She had lived through his defection. After that, handling his return, however unexpected, should be easy.

She arranged a hostess's smile on her face, and ex-tended her right hand graciously. "Hello," she said calmly, and was rewarded by a faint look of surprise in the depths of his eyes. He had expected her to faint, perhaps? She stiffened her resolve, praying that when their hands met she would betray no emotion.

"Welcome to Mount Larkin, Mr...?" She let the sentence drift off.

"Stowe. Roger Stowe," he said, raising one dark eyebrow as though daring her to contradict him. When she didn't, he lifted his hand to accept her handshake. She lowered her eyelids slightly over her gray-green eyes as their fingers met. She had almost forgotten how tanned he was and how hard his long brown fingers were. How warm. He held her hand too long for common civility, but she refused to be the first to let go. It was like an emotional game of chicken. She watched his eyes darken as the warmth increased, knowing hers were doing the same.

She parted her lips to speak, but she couldn't. The sensation was traveling up her arm with the consuming inexorability of a spark following a wire toward dynamite, and she knew the explosion would rock her out of her affected indifference.

Abruptly she pulled her hand away, and his eyes narrowed in triumph.

"Thank you, ma'am," he said with mock courtesy as he moved to one side, shrugging out of his jacket carelessly and hanging it on the brass rack without hesitation, as though the house belonged to him and he had been hanging his things there for decades. How dared he? He, who had been in this house only once in his life—to negotiate the size of his severance check. "I was beginning to wonder whether Mount Larkin actually deserved its reputation for hospitality."

"Oh, I assure you it does, Mr. Stowe." Apparently unable to restrain herself any longer, Lina stepped forward, nodding vigorously so that her long golden curls shone under the foyer chandelier. "Hi. I'm Carolina Travers. I've been here two weeks and I love it. I wish I could stay forever." Especially now that you're here, her dazzling smile added.

Drake turned toward Lina and grinned—not the twisted cold smirk he had given to Amanda, she noticed, but the wide heart-stopping smile she remembered from so long ago. The smile was almost too gorgeous, relieving the bold rugged angles of his face and revealing the unsuspected dimple in his left cheek. Even Lina, an accomplished flirt herself, was blushing under the power of that smile.

"Oh, surely not forever," he corrected her as they shook hands. "You're young, but you must have learned by now that nothing lasts forever."

He was still smiling down at Lina as he spoke, but Amanda felt somehow that there might be a message for her in the words. She even wondered briefly if it might be some kind of apology. Could he have been saying, in essence, that their affair had been just one of those things, a fleeting flame that couldn't have lasted anyway, even if he hadn't been offered a king's ransom to extinguish it?

But then he turned back to Amanda, and his expression showed her immediately how foolish that explanation was. His wide mouth was a grim thin line, his strong square jaw set tight, and his cobalt-blue eyes hard and almost black. She had never seen his eyes like that, even in her nightmares. They had always been full of tenderness and laughter, or fiery with passion. But this was something else, something frightening. This looked like hatred.

"Isn't that right?"

She couldn't answer right away, as though those eyes had blasted the air right out of her lungs. Why hatred? Why should Drake Daniels hate her? He might have hated her grandmother perhaps, who had made it so clear that Mr. Drake Daniels was not good enough to marry a Larkin. But he must know that her grandmother was dead now—had been for five years—and that it was too late to come back looking for revenge. It was too late for anything, really. It was over, long gone. Nothing remained of her teenage passion. And for that she was grateful. That insane passion had almost killed her. It was far smarter to be numb.

"Indeed it is," she finally rejoined casually. "And believe me, Lina, that's as it should be. Forever just might be too long for some things."

Lina looked slightly bemused, and Amanda took advantage of the momentary silence to change the subject. "But come and meet the rest of our household. This is our guest Webster Bronson." The older man nodded, apparently relieved that the glamorous new author was too young to be competition for Cicely. "And this is Tom Wyndham."

Drake shook hands with both men, exchanging light jokes about the miserable weather, and then turned to Cicely. "And of course this is Miss Larkin," he said, his eyes hard again.

Cicely stammered a hello, and Amanda could see that, though her aunt had been struggling silently with her confusion, she didn't yet have her emotions under control.

"I think Mr. Stowe would like to go upstairs," Amanda began, hoping to forestall her aunt's questions, but it was too late.

Her aunt turned from the tall man to her niece and said in a thin voice, "But, Amanda, why are you calling him Mr. Stowe? How can Drake be Roger Stowe? I don't understand."

Amanda squeezed her aunt's hand meaningfully and tried to keep her voice normal. "I don't think Mr. Stowe wants us giving away his secrets. He writes under a pen name, don't you see? He made the reservation under his pen name so that no one would realize who he was."

As she put the situation into words, Amanda felt another spark of fury. Of course that was what he had done. He knew she would never have accepted Drake Daniels as a guest, so he came as Roger Stowe. And now, judging by the awed looks he was getting from everyone, she was going to have to let him stay. She couldn't afford to have her guests reporting to their friends that she had mistreated the charming Roger Stowe. She clenched her fist in impotent rage. What a cheap trick!

Cicely was still frowning and twisting her fingers anxiously. "Is that true, Drake? Are you really Roger Stowe? You really write those murder mysteries?"

He nodded indifferently and brushed back the wet hair that had feathered around his broad forehead. "Surprised, Cicely?" His deep voice was derisive, his smile wicked. "I thought you might be. Your family didn't exactly expect great things from me, did they? 'Wasting away in some picturesque hovel,' is, I believe, how old Mrs. Larkin saw my future."

Really, he had turned into a bully, Amanda thought as she saw her aunt flush. It did sound like the kind of thing Olivia would have said, especially when she had been afraid that Drake wanted to share that "hovel" with Amanda. But it was so long ago. How could he still be so bitter? The Drake Daniels she remembered hadn't ever been bitter or vindictive. Apparently success didn't suit him as well as poverty had. She stepped in quickly, speaking in a parody of Southern gentility.

"And we're all so delighted that you proved us wrong, Mr. Daniels," she purred, hoping he could hear the sarcasm behind the words. "But I know you're eager to get settled in, so why don't you get your things and I'll show you to your room?"

She turned to the others, who were clearly buzzing with curiosity about the startling revelations. "Why don't you all go back and finish breakfast," she suggested, steering her aunt with one hand firmly around her shoulders. "We'll give our new guest some quiet time, and I'm sure he'll join us later."

The men nodded and followed Cicely into the hall, hoping, Amanda felt sure, to coax the whole story out of her, but Lina, who was not accustomed to controlling her impulses, lingered shamelessly.

"This is all so thrilling," she enthused, standing so close that she had to tilt her head back to look up at him. "I can't believe I actually know who Roger Stowe really is. What should I call you—Drake or Roger?"

He appeared to consider, his blue eyes surveying the high foyer, taking in the sparkling chandelier, the graceful sweep of the stairway, the checkerboard marble floors. "I think that at Mount Larkin I should be Drake Daniels,'' he answered finally. ''I wouldn't want to make the Larkins uncomfortable.''

The devil he wouldn't, Amanda thought to herself angrily. That was exactly what he was after—to show the Larkin family that Drake Daniels was every bit as good as they were. Every bit as wealthy. Or perhaps, she amended, in light of the reversal the Larkin meager fortunes had suffered, considerably more so. Though he still wore jeans, the cut and style were obviously expensive, and his black sweater had the extravagant softness of cashmere. The worn basketball shoes were gone, replaced by boots of fine glossy leather. She studied the expert cut of his thick blond hair, and even after a dousing by the rain it looked perfect, a far cry from the shaggy locks she had run her fingers through years ago.

She felt a pinch of longing at her midsection, as though someone had pulled a belt too tight. Dragging her eyes away, she stared out through the side panels, where the rain was still pelting the late-autumn ground. She had to stop looking at him.

Lina, on the other hand, couldn't seem to get enough of him. She had made it as far as the hallway before she turned back for one last sally. ''You must tell us the whole story about how you knew Amanda,'' she urged. ''It sounds exciting.''

Drake glanced at Amanda through dark eyes and then smiled over at Lina. ''Later,'' he said, managing to fill the syllables with promise. When Lina affected a pretty pout of disappointment, he added, ''It'll keep. It's a *very* old story.''

Lina had to accept her dismissal then, and with another shimmer of golden curls she was gone.

Now they were alone. It was a moment Amanda had secretly fantasized about for six long years. How she had craved the chance to confront Drake Daniels, to tell him exactly what she thought of him and his behavior. Now she could drop these ridiculous hostess manners, Amanda told herself as she stared out the window, and demand to know why in blazes he was here.

But strangely she couldn't do it. Though she hated to admit it, her fantasies had always ended the same way, with her beating her fists on his hard golden chest, crying out the anguish of the horrible years, and him holding her tightly, explaining, soothing, kissing away her tears. Instinctively she knew that could never happen now. He had changed too much. Maybe she had, too.

The polished handsome man who stood behind her now was just too different from the man who had betrayed her. In spite of everything that had once been between them, this man was a stranger to her, and all the accusations she had stored up were powerless against the contempt she felt from him.

So she kept her back to him. The rain was easing, though the sky was still smoky with clouds, and she watched as the last sparkling drops trickled down the windowpanes, collecting in the beveled corners and disappearing.

"It's letting up, I think," she said finally, without turning around. "I'll help you with your bags."

"Fine." His voice was flatly acquiescent.

But neither of them moved. It was as if they both knew there were things that must be said before they could take up this new relationship—that of hostess and guest. Something had to be said to put an end to the old relationship—that of a foolish girl and her fickle lover. But what were the magic words that could do that? "I'm sorry I let them buy me off?—" and "oh, that's okay?" No—she didn't know any words powerful enough to neutralize the acid of their past.

Confused, she put her hand up to trace the path of a languidly descending raindrop. As she did so, her focus adjusted, and instead of seeing the wet trail she saw the watery reflection of the foyer behind her, where he stood tall and still, facing her. Her finger appeared to be touching his body, and she pulled it away with a muffled cry.

His reflection moved then, coming slowly closer until it blurred and blended with hers. He stopped right behind her, the heat of his body warming her shoulder blades even through their woolen sweaters. Still he didn't speak, and she felt her heart speed up, like an engine fueled by the warmth of his body. A small circle of condensation formed on the window. She must have been breathing shallowly through her mouth.

Embarrassed, she clamped her lips shut and forced herself to breathe deeply, hoping he wouldn't notice the foggy proof of her susceptibility. It was humiliating that his mere presence could reduce her to this.

But of course he did notice. He raised his arm over her shoulder, holding it so close to her face that the softness of the black wool feathered her cheek. With a strong forefinger, he pulled a slow thick line through the circle wordlessly.

He gave a malicious chuckle and let his hand fall to the doorknob. "Shall we go, then?"

She felt herself blushing and was glad that her back was to him. Had she really been hoping he would touch her, that he would be as affected by her presence as she was by his? Then she was a fool! This was just a game to him. He had stripped away her veneer of indifference as easily as a spoiled little boy might rip apart a toy to see what made it work. And then, bored, he had carelessly tossed the toy aside.

She didn't know why it should surprise her. He had done the same thing before. She reached up and wiped the last drops of condensation away with her hand. "Sure. Let's go."

They went outside and walked together in silence, the leaves crunching soggily under their boots as they doubled around the side of the house. She was glad she had done her exercises this morning, so that her right leg was feeling limber and any slight hesitancy in her walk could be put down to caution. He was walking slowly, too, apparently remembering that Georgia clay was treacherous when it was wet.

Thunder still rumbled in the middle distance, and she felt the wet air seep through her sweater. They should have gone through the kitchen, where she could have picked up a parka. But she had instinctively wanted to avoid meeting the others again so soon. She glanced up at him as he walked just a pace ahead of her. He hadn't put his jacket back on, either, and his broad shoulders and muscular arms stretched the wool of his sweater. He obviously hadn't been leading a sedentary writer's life. She wondered what he did to stay so firm, now that he wasn't mowing lawns anymore.

They passed under a towering pine, and his shoulder jostled a low-hanging cluster of needles, sending a shower of cold raindrops splattering across her face.

"Ugh," she complained, stopping and wiping futilely at her drenched skin. "Be careful!"

"Sorry," he said politely and, pulling a white handkerchief from his back pocket, swabbed at her cheeks. Drops had caught in her eyelashes, glittering like tears, and he brushed them away with a light touch.

"I can do that," she said waspishly, whipping the handkerchief from his hand and blotting her face violently. She didn't want him touching her. Not even for such practical purposes. Not even through the barrier of linen. "And watch out next time, won't you? Don't forget how tall you are. We only trim up to six feet around here."

"Yes, ma'am," he said, leaning back against the tree, lazily obedient, to watch her. "No need to get so heated up. It wasn't deliberate, you know. If I wanted to get hold of you, I'd be much more direct about it."

His eyes were openly assessing her, and in spite of her anger she found herself wondering what he thought of what he saw. It had been six years—and she had passed from a girl to a woman, even to a mother, during that time. Her coltish figure had finally filled out, as was all too evident now that the wet air had molded her sweater to her body, and she knew that, at twenty-five, she was very different from the teenager he had known.

But he was different, too, physically as well as emotionally. He was...sophisticated, she supposed. The younger Drake Daniels had been anything but. He had been roughly tanned and sensual in a much more primitive way when he'd come to work on the Mount Larkin property six years ago. His torn and beltless jeans had ridden low on his lean hips, and his shirtless torso had gleamed with sweat in the relentless summer sun. He had always smelled of hot grass then, and she'd found it an intoxicating perfume.

"Oh, really?" she countered finally, drawing herself up as straight as she could and wishing her wet sweater were less revealing. She felt her palms itching to slap that arrogantly appraising look off his face, but she settled for adding tartly, "Well, if you were, I can promise you that my reaction would be much more direct, as well."

He chuckled, but his eyes were still hard as they moved up and down her body. "I said 'if,' Amanda. *If* I wanted you. And you can unclench your pretty little fists, because I can assure you I do not."

Her cheeks tingled, and a blast of heat shot through her, just as if she'd been slapped. But she mustn't let him know that. She lifted her chin and handed him his handkerchief. "Fine," she said, her voice clipped and tight. "So perhaps you wouldn't mind telling me just what the hell you *are* doing here? My grandmother offered a pretty penny to get you out of here—more pennies than she could afford, as it turned out. And you were supposed to stay out. Why didn't you?"

"Hmm," he said thoughtfully, folding the white cloth as he began to walk again. "Curiosity, I guess." He broke a dead twig from a maple and snapped it into short pieces. "I guess that's as good a word as any."

They rounded the back of the house, where he had parked his car. Amanda was still a pace or two behind him but listening intently. Was that all? He wasn't going to offer any more explanation than that?

He reached into his jeans pocket and pulled out a set of car keys. He jammed one into the lock of his trunk, the violence of his movements at variance with the conversational tone of his voice. He twisted the key roughly and threw open the trunk.

Amanda watched, frowning. "How—" she began.

But he didn't intend to let her speak. Bracing one leather-shod foot on the fender, he began pulling pigskin suitcases out, biting out his next words between lifts. "Who does your lawn now, Amanda? Is there some new young man who attends to your—" he snapped the trunk shut and looked at her insolently "—needs?"

Amanda nearly gasped, shocked by the frontal attack. "Our needs are met perfectly well," she said quellingly.

"Really?" His eyes scanned the property, and she flushed as she watched him register the changes. In Olivia's time the entire four acres had been formally sculpted. Today they had to make do only with landscaping around the house and letting the rest run wild. His gaze stopped at the white sign that announced Mount Larkin Bed and Breakfast. "Things look a little...neglected to me."

His blue eyes, tilted slightly with amusement, were on her. He seemed to be waiting for her response, probably hoping she'd show some embarrassment. His elbow rested nonchalantly on the roof of the car. For the first time she noticed the car. The bunged-up little economy car had gone the way of the tattered blue jeans. Mr. Roger Stowe, author, drove a car more fitting his new life-style—a red Jaguar sports car. Its sleek lines undulated, the gleaming paint job catching the feeble rays of the tentative December sun and magnifying them.

One look at the car confirmed her earlier suspicions. Whatever other reasons he might give, Drake Daniels had really come here to gloat. To show off, to laugh, perhaps, at how the mighty had fallen.

It made her feel slightly sick, and she fought back a rush of disappointment. It was just plain cruel, something she would have sworn Drake could never be. She had told herself he had taken the money out of desperation, that he was poor. She had been pathetic in her misery, rationalizing with every clichéd excuse in the book. Maybe his mother was sick. Maybe his sister needed an operation. Someday he would explain.

But someday had come, and he clearly had no intention of explaining. He didn't even think he needed to. He was proud of his shrewd business deal and cruelly amused that her fortunes had not turned out so well.

The disillusionment was bitter, and she said the first hurtful thing that occurred to her.

"Oh, dear, I do hope you're not thinking of applying for the job yourself," she said in mock concern, running her fingers along the curving corners of the Jaguar. She shot him a nasty smile. "It's not that your work wasn't adequate, of course. We just found your prices a bit . . . exorbitant."

Gratified to see that the smug smile had dropped from his lips, she turned her back on him, moving with as much poise as she could toward the kitchen door. "It's a marvelous car you've got there, Drake. Too bad my grandmother isn't alive to see how well her expensive lawn boy turned out."

CHAPTER THREE

THE FLOUR PUFFED UP in small circles around Amanda's hands as she pummeled the dough savagely. It was midafternoon. What had they been doing in there all these hours? As Lina's laughter spilled from the closed doors of the parlor, followed closely by Drake's throaty chuckle, she again pounded the bread with her fist, this time so hard that the soft edge of her hand was bruised against the counter tiles. Whatever Lina and Drake were doing, they seemed to be hitting it off famously.

But then, why shouldn't they? Amanda licked a powdery film of flour off her lips and blew lightly at a wisp of hair that had fallen into her eyes. She knew all too well how charming Drake could be when he put his mind to it. Especially to a very young romantic girl. Perhaps she should drop Lina a word of warning. No. Lina was twenty-two years old, well past the age of consent. If she wanted to twitter with Drake Daniels all through dinner, and even until the sun came up, it was no business of Amanda's. Trying to tune out the sounds from the other room, she redoubled her efforts on the dough.

When her arms began to ache, she stopped briefly and bent to check on the loaf that was still in the oven. It would be ready soon, and she considered whether to start yet another loaf. She had decided to bake—next to painting it was the best therapy—because she was too keyed up to socialize with the others. Even a long cozy call from Julie earlier that afternoon hadn't helped her to relax. The giggling stories of Mickey Mouse and Cinderella's castle had only intensified her longing for her daughter, and she even briefly considered catching the next plane to Florida to join Julie at Disney World.

But she knew she couldn't leave Cicely with a household of guests—especially not when Drake was one of them—so she controlled the impulse. Hanging up had been difficult. She had reminded her stepson, Martin Hamilton, at least ten times to give Julie her vitamins—so often in fact that even the easygoing Martin had asked if she was okay. She had said yes, of course, but was she? If she was this nervous already on day one, could she really bear having Drake in the house for a whole week?

As the giggling continued, she decided against baking a fourth loaf. She was good and tired of listening to Lina's ecstasies. As soon as this new loaf was ready she could go out into the garden with her chalks and leave them to their flirtation.

Suddenly the kitchen door swung open and she straightened up hurriedly, rubbing her floury hands on her white apron and hoping her cheeks weren't too flushed from the heat of the stove. But it was only Cicely.

"Hi." Wondering why she felt a twinge of disappointment, Amanda turned back to the waiting dough and began to braid it carefully. "Hungry? It's still a while till dinner. Sit down just a second and I'll get you some milk as soon as I pop this in the oven.''

"That's okay. I'll get it."

Gratefully, Amanda heard her aunt's soft slippers cross the floor toward the refrigerator. She needed time to relax. She breathed deeply and arranged her face in calmer lines. She mustn't worry Cicely, especially as she had spent all morning assuring her aunt that she could handle Drake Daniels's presence perfectly well.

"Are you on your *third* loaf, Amanda?" Her aunt had joined her at the stove and was pouring milk into a small saucepan. "Why so many? Are we expecting any extra guests tomorrow? Like the twenty-third battalion, perhaps?"

Amanda looked up quickly, her hands still busy braiding. Such a jocular tone was unusual for her aunt. In spite of her own tension Amanda had to smile at the sparkle she saw in the older woman's soft gray eyes. Her lunch out with Webster must have been pleasant indeed.

"No, no new guests," Amanda countered mischievously. "It's just that I hear love makes people extremely hungry and I thought I'd better be prepared." She bumped her aunt playfully with her hip, nudging her out of the way as she opened the oven door to switch loaves.

She had just slid the new loaf in when a fresh peal of laughter rang out from the parlor. "Oh, Drake," she heard Lina bubble, "I'm so glad you came."

Amanda and her aunt exchanged looks. "Hmm...I wonder how many pieces of your fresh bread Carolina will want in the morning?" her aunt mused with studied carelessness, avoiding her niece's eyes by assiduously stirring her milk.

"Thousands," Amanda answered tersely. She knew where her aunt was heading, and she anticipated the next comment. "The important question is, how hungry will Mr. Stowe-Daniels be?" She turned on the faucet full force, the rush of hot water effectively drowning out any sounds from the other room, and added dryly, "My guess is that he'll be able to skip breakfast altogether."

Cicely nodded. "I think so, too, and that worries me, Mandy." She poured her milk into a glass and sat down at the big table. "He's too old for her. He's in his thirties now, isn't he? But it's not just his age. He's too..." She seemed to flounder, swirling the contents of her glass in small circles as she searched for the right adjective. "Too—"

"I know," Amanda broke in impatiently. "*Too smooth. Too sleek*. He's too everything. I've noticed."

"Well, the thing is, Carolina's mother trusts me to keep her out of trouble. I know we're not supposed to concern ourselves with the private lives of our guests, but really, Carolina isn't just any guest, and I don't think it's right to let her be swept off her feet by a man who couldn't possibly take her seriously." Cicely sipped at the milk, her sparkly mood gone, replaced by the more customary worried frown. "I hate to do it, but I feel I should say something to her mother."

Amanda scrubbed at a bowl vigorously before speaking. "My goodness," she said finally, unable to keep the edge of bitterness out of her voice, "this sounds all too familiar."

The minute the words were out of her mouth she regretted them, and she turned an apologetic look toward her aunt. She had promised herself she'd never again reproach Cicely about that subject. God knows she had said enough to her the night Drake left—sobbing, furious things they would never forget.

She saw the distress reflected in Cicely's eyes and reproached herself for her lack of restraint. Her aunt was a gentle woman, a little timid perhaps, and not as good at keeping a secret as she might be, but that was because she herself had no guile or deceit. She had meant well when she had spilled Amanda's secret to Olivia Larkin. If tragedy had come of it, Drake Daniels was to blame, not poor Cicely.

With an iron will Amanda had kept her vow of silence, for six years had choked back the resentment at having been betrayed, refusing to speak the angry words until, denied any outlet, the anger had finally died.

Or so she had thought, until he'd come back this morning. Now, like monsters in a B-grade movie, the emotions were beginning to wriggle with new life. Wasn't it just like Drake. He hadn't been under their roof for twenty-four hours and already he had begun to sow discord.

She twisted off the faucet and, drying her hands on her apron, went over to give her aunt a hug.

"It's okay, Cicely. You're right. You were right about Drake before, and you're right now. I'll tell you what." She knelt beside the table and took her aunt's hands in her own. They felt paper-thin but warm, and a rush of protective love for her swept over Amanda. "Before you go and get Lina's mother upset, let me talk to Drake. He probably thinks Lina's a lot more experienced than she is." She laughed, hoping her light attitude would coax the anxiety out of her aunt's face. "Lina puts up a rather flashy front, you know, with those eyelashes going a mile a minute, and she's really been turning it on for him. You weren't here for lunch, so you didn't see it."

In spite of her laughter, Amanda's stomach tightened at the memory of lunch. It had been punctuated with Lina's effusive trills of laughter, as though every word out of Drake's mouth had been a gem of wit and brilliance. Amanda had felt, in the presence of buoyant naïveté, more like a spinster aunt herself, like a schoolmarm scowling down on rambunctious teens.

She had tried to remember whether she, too, had hung on Drake's every word all those years ago. Probably so, she decided, staring down at her plate as the shame of the memory stained her cheeks. He had been the most intelligent, exciting, sensual man she'd ever set eyes on, and she had fallen hard. Even harder than Lina had today.

Her aunt looked sad. "I know," she admitted, shaking her head. "I guess the truth is that it isn't really Carolina I'm worried about. It's you." She peered anxiously into Amanda's eyes. "You look strained, honey. I know you said you'd be okay, but I don't see how. Maybe I should ask him to leave—I just don't know. Do you think he would? Do you think it would help to talk to Drake about something like that?"

"I don't think so," Amanda answered, attempting to keep the bitterness out of her voice. "But we can try it as a last resort. Just let *me* talk to Drake first, okay?''

She heard more laughter and realized with a spurt of anger that she couldn't listen to another minute of it. "Keep an eye on this last loaf for me, will you, Cicely?" She saw her aunt's bewildered nod before she flung down her quilted oven pad and, grabbing up her box of chalks, pushed roughly through the kitchen door.

TWO HOURS LATER, she still sat in the pond garden knowing she should go inside. The turkey needed basting; the cranberry needed slicing. Everyone would be getting hungry. Soon, she promised her conscience. Soon she would gather up her chalks and her tablets and be practical again.

But not yet. She dropped the moss-green chalk she had been using to sketch the weathered cupid that stood guard over the pond and leaned back against the chilled wrought iron of her bench. It was getting very cold. Her breath hung in a milky mist, and her cheeks were tight and numb from the wind.

But she didn't go in. The sky had cleared, and the afternoon was, in spite of the cold and the approaching darkness, simply too beautiful. The sun had lowered itself behind the trees, and their bare branches seemed to end in flaming torches of sunset. Some of that fire had spilled into the mossy rectangle of the pond, too, and it burned at her feet like a caldron.

The entire garden, bathed like this in honey light, seemed a magical place, and like a superstitious child, she was reluctant to leave its protection.

But what exactly did she need protection against? Drake? Why? It was over between them, in spite of the way her body had reacted to the sight of him this morning, in spite of the jealousy that had stabbed so fiercely in the kitchen just now. That had meant nothing, she told herself fiercely, rubbing her hands together to fight the growing chill. She had read that an amputee will sometimes feel pain in a limb long gone—and today's aching need had been like that. A ghost pain.

Still, it hurt. She sighed, and her breath lingered near her lips like a snowy kiss.

"Hiding?"

She had been so long alone that the voice shocked her, and her heart lurched as she lifted her head.

"Drake!" With the rays of the setting sun flooding over him, he looked more like a golden statue than a man. A statue of a gladiator perhaps, she thought, still fanciful from her hours of solitude. His suede jacket rode his broad shoulders like a coat of burnished golden armor, and his long muscular legs were planted slightly apart in a posture of dominance.

"Your aunt sent me to find you," he said calmly, as though that were normal. "Something about turkey juice."

She smiled in spite of herself. "Gravy," she corrected.

He moved then, and her fancy switched images, from gladiator to archangel. His hair, sparked by the sun to a red-gold as deep as a fire opal, looked like a halo. Scooting her leg out of the way, he eased down onto the bench beside her.

Her body reacted instantly to his proximity, rushing a shivering heat through her that, as it encountered her chilled skin, resulted in an explosion of goose bumps. But he didn't seem to notice. He looked comfortable on the hard bench and seemed willing to wait for her to speak first.

She on the other hand was no longer comfortable at all and had no idea what to say. How had he known to look for her here? They had never come here together, preferring at first to let their innocent love romp in the sun-dappled fringes of the Larkin property. And then later, when innocence had died giving birth to passion, this small garden had been too restrained, too formal. They had needed something wilder, with wider sweep.

She shook the idea out of her mind and rubbed the goose bumps from her arms. Of course he knew this place. He had known every inch of Larkin property back then. As a junior member of the landscaping crew, it might well have been his unlucky assignment to scrape moss from the cupid's sad eyes and scoop dead wisteria vines from the murky pond.

"So, *are* you hiding?" Though his face was cast in shadows, his voice had a smile in it. "Are you AWOL from turkey duty?"

"Of course not," she said, pushing away the uncomfortably vivid image of his young body bending over the water, his back bare and bronze, his arms wet and glistening up to the elbows. "I'm just enjoying a little quiet time."

He grinned. "Sounds like the same thing to me. And I have to say I don't blame you. Every five minutes back at the house somebody calls frantically for you.''

Amanda groaned. "Anything urgent?"

He laughed. "Well, they seem to think so. Carolina wants you to help her decide between a turquoise ribbon and an aqua one. Wyndham wants you to admire his picture, which, by the way, looks like mud with leaves in it. Your aunt keeps predicting that the turkey will dry out, managing to make it sound like a disaster of cosmic proportions. Even Bronson is asking where you are, though he doesn't say why. It's a madhouse.''

She buried her head in her arm and chuckled. "No, it's just a typical day at Mount Larkin. I suppose I'd better go on in." But she didn't stand up.

Neither did Drake. They sat in a strained silence a few minutes, listening to the evening wind slip through the tall pines, and then he leaned over and picked up her cupid sketch.

"This is nice," he said slowly. "A little mournful, perhaps, but powerful. You've become very good, haven't you? Your pictures were always pretty, but I've been looking over some of them up at the house, and your talent has matured considerably.''

She was glad the shadows hid her blush of pleasure. "Well, getting older is something that we all do, so I can't take any credit for that.''

"I didn't say get older," he corrected. "I said mature. And you're not taking a compliment very gracefully. Just say 'thank you.''"

"Thanks," she murmured, and bent to gather her things.

"Accepting compliments well is an art, they tell me." Leaning back, he crossed his long legs in front of him. "For instance, I've learned to say 'thank you' quite politely myself, when people tell me they enjoy Roger Stowe murder mysteries." His voice was teasing. "I noticed you have both books in your downstairs library. Want to test my manners?"

"I can already tell your humility needs a little work," she countered acerbically, still tossing chalks into her box. "But yes, I've read them. And enjoyed them. Now say 'thank you.'"

"Thank you, ma'am," he said dryly. "But is that the best you can do?"

All the chalks and cloths and pencils were finally put away, and she snapped her case shut. "You don't need me to tell you the books are good, Drake. You've got the *New York Times* to do that. And newspapers all over the country. Why, the reviewer for our paper came right out and admitted your love scenes curled her toes."

She rested the case on her lap and met his eyes. "Anyhow, I'm sure the royalty checks speak louder than words. So you obviously don't need my little compliments."

"Don't I?" He leaned forward, resting his elbows on his knees and letting his hands dangle loosely near her legs. "I'm disappointed. You used to be more generous with your praise."

Yes, she remembered, she certainly had been. All those years ago, and it seemed like only yesterday. She had sat for hours sketching his strong hands, or his heart-stopping profile, or even the absorbed curve of his beautifully shaped back as he bent over the typewriter. And then they would read over his work together, curled together spoon-style on the tiny sofa. How rapturous she had been! As unguarded as Lina, she had used every superlative at her command—"the most talented, the cleverest, the smartest, the funniest . . ."

And then, as though bored by the list of his virtues, or perhaps maddened by the feel of her body molded against him, he would toss the papers recklessly on the floor beside them, and turn her face to his . . .

"Yes, well, as you say, I've matured since then." She wondered why she couldn't bring herself to tell him the truth—that she adored his books and that she respected his writing even more now than she had six years ago. Had she really grown so pinched of heart that she would begrudge him the praise he deserved? She wasn't proud of her miserliness—and yet she couldn't tell him. She wasn't going to be an easy ego trip for him this time.

Instead she looked at the fading garden around them. The golden light had deepened to crimson, and though she was unreasonably reluctant to do so, she knew she must go in.

"Well, time to get back to work," she sighed, tying the ribbons of her portfolio into a quick bow.

"Must we? Oh, damn, I forgot entirely what I came out here to do!" he exclaimed irritably, slapping his jacket pocket. "Your aunt wanted me to give you this letter. She said you'd been waiting for it." His hand disappeared into the suede jacket and came out holding a long white envelope.

Recognizing her stepson's handwriting, Amanda laughed delightedly and reached eagerly for the letter.

"Oh, wonderful," she said. "I hoped it would come today."

He watched as she ripped open the envelope and quickly ran through the preface from Martin, which assured her that everything was going well, aside from some predictable homesickness, and that they were all looking forward to spending Christmas together.

Then, ignoring Drake's silent scrutiny, she devoured the short but ineffably sweet sentences from Julie. It had been dictated to Martin, of course, but the sight of the familiar shaky signature brought happy tears to Amanda's eyes.

I miss you, Mommy. Our house is prettier than Cinderella's Castle. I think I'll write a story about our house when I get back. Is it snowing? I want a sled for Christmas.

Love, Julie

Amanda held the letter tightly, fighting back the rush of loneliness that threatened to overwhelm her. The simple words had for just a moment brought her daughter back to her. She didn't see how she could wait another two weeks to hold Julie again. Phone calls just weren't enough.

"Not bad news, I hope?" Not until Drake's voice interrupted her thoughts did she stop to think how tense she must appear, clutching the letter and blinking back tears.

"Oh, no, no," she assured him. "Everything is fine. It's just a letter from Julie—" She looked up, remembering that they had never spoken of Julie before. "My daughter," she added awkwardly.

Was it just the ever-darkening sky or did his face really look harder now? "Yes, I've gathered that you have a child. Webster tells me she's visiting her brother—her half brother, that is."

"Yes, that's right. Richard's son from his first marriage. Martin's a doctor—he's doing his residency down in Florida, and every year around this time Julie goes for a long visit. She calls him Uncle Martin and she's quite fond of him. He takes her to Disney World and Sea World and the beaches."

She was talking too much. She always talked too much when she was nervous. Did he remember that? She tried to slow down. "This may be the last year she can take the time off from school, so she's staying a little longer than usual, and I guess I'm just missing her, that's all."

He paused a moment, and then his voice was deep. "How old is she?"

The fear that had been coiled in the pit of her stomach rose, and she swallowed hard to force it back. Please god, she prayed, let me say this right.

"She's just turned five," she said. "She started kindergarten this year, and she feels quite grown up. But she's one of the youngest in her class, really. Here you have to turn five by September the first to be admitted into kindergarten, and she just barely made it."

There was a heavy pause, during which she wondered anxiously whether she had overdone it. Perhaps she shouldn't have added the part about the admissions cutoff date. Maybe it sounded as though she were rubbing his face in it.

Or maybe he was counting. That would be all right. But the silence stretched on, and a flicker of new apprehension went through her. It couldn't possibly take this long to count to nine—what was he thinking about?

"Well," he said finally, and his voice was utterly flat. "You and Hamilton didn't waste any time, did you?"

She breathed deeply and stood up. "Well, we couldn't really," she said, her nerves making her chatter as foolishly as Julie might. "You see, we knew Richard was sick—we didn't have a lot of time."

Because her right leg was stiff from sitting in the damp cold so long, she walked slowly, too self-conscious to look at him. She had gone several yards before she realized he wasn't following. Stopping, she looked back at him.

"Coming?"

"You knew Hamilton was dying when you married him?" He spoke slowly, as though disbelieving.

"Why...yes." She stumbled over the words, uncertain where the conversation was going. Had she revealed something she shouldn't have? The whole thing was so complicated that it was difficult to maneuver safely. "Yes. He had a muscular disease and we knew he couldn't live long."

"Mandy..." He leaned forward, as though to come to her, then checked himself, but she heard the bewildered compassion that had, for the two short syllables, filled his voice.

His anger and contempt she could handle, but the softness caught her off guard. With a flood of hot dismay rushing through her, she stared at him through the dusk. He was just a man again. No more fiery light poured through the trees to light his hair into a halo—

even the gold of his jacket had dimmed to a muddy brown.

And yet, she realized with an alarming tumble of her heart, he was just as dizzyingly handsome in dull shadows as he had been standing in the throbbing glow of the sunset. And she felt the same way about him.

No, she told herself, as the ache she had felt earlier began to build again. No! Just a ghost pain. He has been amputated from your life. But the pain in her stomach spread out in concentric circles, until soon her hands were too weak to make a fist.

Please, no, she thought, disoriented by the piercing desire and reaching out to steady herself on the rough trunk of a pine. She couldn't let this happen. Desperately she dug into the bitter bag of epithets she had kept handy all these years, and flung them out like old rags to smother the raging fire in her heart. Remember—he is a liar, a cheat. A gigolo. An extortionist. But the fire was out of control, and it effortlessly consumed the words, leaving her nothing to fight with.

Dark or light, good or bad, he was still the man she loved.

CHAPTER FOUR

LOST IN THE NUMBING realization, she didn't hear his next quietly spoken question, and he had to repeat it.

"You knew he was dying—and you married him anyway?"

"Yes, of course," she answered dully.

"Why?"

She tried for just a second to think up a convincing lie. But with the new awareness heavy on her mind she found it impossible. With a resigned flutter of her hand, she turned away without answering. Maybe tomorrow she could think of something. Tonight she was tired of lying.

But suddenly she whipped around, turning so fast her long ponytail stung her neck. She didn't have to lie. The truth, just this once, would suffice. He would never know what she really meant.

And so she told it.

"When you love somebody, nothing else matters," she whispered, and the earnest sound carried through the clear cold night to where he stood, a shadow among shadows. "Nothing—nothing they are and nothing they've done. Not even that there can be no future for you."

It was too dark to see his eyes, but the silence was somehow colder than ever.

"I see." His words fell into the chill air like small stones. "And your grandmother and aunt? Did they welcome your new husband? Or did he have to use the back door, too?"

Obviously his mellow mood had vanished. She wondered why. Perhaps it was being out here—a guest, where once he had been only the hired hand. It had been hard for him at the time. "I won't be a gardener forever, Mandy," he had harshly vowed as they lay together on the grass. And he'd kept that promise, if not the others, but apparently the memory of his days of servitude still disturbed him.

"Well, you used the front door today," she said dryly, ignoring his questions, which were obviously just bitter rhetoric. She didn't want to stay here any longer. She found she dreaded this new bitterness as much as she'd earlier feared his softness.

"Much to your aunt's surprise," he said, laughing mirthlessly. He hitched one leg over the other and settled his chin against the back of his hand. "Do you know," he said conversationally, "I think she's scared of me? Should I be insulted or flattered?"

"Neither," she responded flatly. "You should be ashamed." She came closer and stood squarely in front of him, her gray-green eyes dark with anger as they ran contemptuously over his lean form. His clothes had obviously cost a fortune and were designed to make the most of his muscular good looks. But she had liked him better in rags. At least then he'd had integrity. "You slide in here under an assumed name, knowing you would not have been admitted under your own, and then bully a woman you know is not as strong as you are."

He grinned again, showing his dimple, and raised dark brows questioningly. "Not you, surely?"

"Of course not," she spat back. This wasn't going to be easy. Apparently he was determined to be personal.

"I didn't think so," he answered. "You look pretty tough to me." He openly returned her scrutiny, letting his dark blue eyes roam freely over her body. Unfortunately, now that she had added the white apron to her outfit, she knew she must look more like the upstairs maid than the lady of the house.

She accepted his perusal with as much hauteur as she could manage, although she could tell by the throbbing heat below her eyes that her high cheekbones were scarlet.

"So," he drawled, as his eyes came back to her face, "have you decided to warn me about this? To be better behaved around your aunt? You haven't forgotten that I'm not a blue blood, have you, Mandy? I'm just a nobody from nowhere who forgot his place." He brushed a speck from his impeccable trousers. "And in all these years I still haven't learned how to be a good little yard boy."

Her grandmother's voice again. If Olivia had actually said such cutting things to him, Amanda thought suddenly, then she could almost understand why he had gone after the money. Almost. But she could never understand, or forgive, the way he had made love to her first. He had, with infinite expertise, guided her into a world of sensual abandonment, had taught her the unparalleled joy possible when a woman gives herself body and soul to a man. And it hadn't even been necessary. Her grandmother had already been nervous enough to buy him off. He could have had the money, anyhow. It was greedy and cruel to take her soul, too.

"It's not a warning. It's perhaps a gentle reminder to watch your manners." Remembered pain scored her voice, spoiling the desired casual effect, and she moved back nervously against the trees. Pressing her palms against the rough bark, she continued, "And while we're on the subject, I wanted to talk to you about Lina, too."

"Ahh." His response was slow and knowing. "She's a darling, isn't she? She reminds me of you." He swung his leg back down and, putting his hands in his pockets, sauntered toward her. "Of you six years ago, that is. Did you know she writes poetry?"

Though it was scraping her tender skin, Amanda rubbed her hands on the tree rhythmically, unconsciously, as if it were a worry stone and she a meditating monk. As if she could withdraw into herself, protect herself against his nearness. "Of course I know that," she said dismissively. What did this have to do with anything? But in spite of herself she added, "I didn't write poetry."

"No," he agreed, his eyes almost black as he watched her hands slide back and forth across the bark. "But you had poetry in you. It came out in your painting. And you made love like poetry. Don't you remember?"

"Yes . . ." That wasn't what she had meant to say, but she wasn't thinking clearly. She felt suddenly as though she were standing over an open flame, with intense melting heat rising through her legs and into her body. And yet he hadn't so much as touched her.

His hands were still bunched in his pockets. She could see the way the denim stretched across his knuckles.

"I mean, no." Burning hot, she moved backward, trying to escape the flame.

He smiled. "No?"

She gripped the tree as hard as she could, pressing it against her aching chest. "I mean—I mean that has nothing to do with what we're talking about. We're talking about Lina."

He tilted his head, the final light of day picking out strands of fire in his blond hair. "Oh, that's right. Let's see . . . you were about to ask me whether I have any plans to help Lina with her poetry?"

His grin was insulting—to her and to Lina. Amanda felt her temper build like a volcano swelling toward an eruption.

"No, dammit. I wanted to ask you to be fair with Lina. She's a good kid. But she's just that—a kid."

"She's older than you were when I met you."

"I know, but you're older now, too. You're so much more sophisticated than she is. You're so much—" She hated to tell him what she really thought of his transformation. His ego was already insufferably inflated. He'd probably take it as a compliment if she told him that he now wore the sleek confidence of success like ermine robes, and that his casual cynicism and lazy indifference would appear irresistibly sophisticated to one as naive as Lina. "Older," she finished, knowing it was inadequate.

His eyes narrowed. "Really? Somehow it seems to me you're not the one to criticize. Your guests have already filled me in on the widow Hamilton, née Larkin. They tell me your late husband was more than twice your age. Since I'm only ten years older than Lina—well, comparatively speaking, I'm just a lad."

She pushed her fist against the trunk, breaking off a shard of bark with the angry force. "Will you stop bringing this conversation back to me? My marriage has nothing on earth to do with Lina. Or with you. I'm simply asking you to respect my wishes enough to be careful with a friend. She deserves better than to be just grist for a love scene in the next Roger Stowe book."

"What a cynic you've become, Mandy. I wouldn't have expected that." His voice was almost ugly, tight and acid. He flashed a hand out to ruffle one corner of her apron. "And such a domestic, too. You certainly didn't learn that as a child. I seem to remember no fewer than three kitchen servants in those days." She kept her eyes averted. Hearing the bitterness in his voice was enough; she didn't want to see it in his face, as well. "Did you learn to cook when you married the good doctor?"

"Yes," she said, clipping the word.

"Then you didn't live here?"

"Of course not," she responded tartly. "As a matter of fact, Richard did have a house here in Atlanta. But we traveled a lot. We lived in Switzerland for a while." Because Drake's sarcasm had offended her, she didn't add that the traveling had been in search of a cure for Richard's muscle-destroying disease. They had heard of snake-venom cures in South America, and oxygen treatments at a spa in Switzerland. Richard had hated to deplete his savings, hoping to have something to leave her, but she had insisted that they try every avenue. Richard *had* been a good doctor, but more than that he had been a good man.

"How lovely for you," Drake's drawl had a slightly sardonic sound, and she watched his eyes suspiciously as they narrowed to blue velvet pinpoints. "Is that how you hurt your leg? Skiing tumble in the Swiss Alps?"

Her mouth opened and she colored fiercely. She had hoped he hadn't noticed.

"Oh, yes," he said relentlessly. "I noticed. You see, I remember everything about you. I even remember exactly how you used to walk. Something's wrong, just ever so slightly wrong, with your right leg."

As she stared into his smug face, she thought of the long crazy descent down the hill, the breathless last struggle that had ended in pain and failure. Never would she tell him how she had chased him that night, how she had been willing to beg him to take her with him, even though she knew he had just sold her for ten thousand dollars. Never.

"More like a hill, really," she said with assumed carelessness, eschewing an outright lie but confident that his prejudice would keep him from wondering what she meant.

And she was right. He made a short sound, like a snort of disgust, and then he smiled coldly again. "It sounds like a glamorous life. You wouldn't have lived on the continent if you'd been married to a struggling author, would you? Just think of all the hassles you missed—the clothes dripping on the line, the coupons clipped out of the papers, the TV dinners, the squalling babies with no nanny to feed them...."

She shrugged, as though she hadn't ever given it a thought, but the images pained her. Once upon a time, she would have done anything to be the one who fixed his TV dinners. And the babies... She couldn't even think about it.

She turned her back to him without answering. She should have gone inside long ago. This conversation had to stop before it got out of control. But before she took two steps, his hands were on her shoulders, pulling her roughly around to face him.

"But there's something else you missed out on, isn't there, Mandy?" He dragged her up against his body, pressing soft chest against hard chest until she could feel his heartbeat virtually pulsing into her oversensitive breast. His fingers dug into the soft skin of her upper arms, and her legs gave way under her as she stared helplessly into his black-fringed eyes.

"You also missed this," he growled, and his hard mouth took hers in savage possession. She felt the bite of the tree against her back as his body crushed her against it. The soft cashmere and suede of his clothing could not disguise the fierce strength of the body beneath. His long hard thighs imprisoned her so that she could not fight against the bruising primitive demands of his mouth and hands.

It was as though she were being sucked down into a black whirlpool, and she felt a sickening lurch as she fought the fall. She clung to the edge of rational thought as long as she could, but all too soon she felt her grip slipping.

And then it wasn't falling at all. It was soaring. She clung to his broad shoulders and let the thrill wash over her. Oh, yes, this was love—she remembered it well. Her mind, perhaps, had tried to forget the afternoons they had spent together on the far edge of the Larkin property, with summer grass for sheets and a fallen log for a pillow, but her body had never forgotten. In this instant, with one kiss to guide it, her body had recognized his, the way a flower recognizes the sun, and was opening toward it, reaching for it, blooming under it.

"Drake," she whispered into the fire of his hair, as his lips moved to pour kisses down the tender column of her throat. It had been so long. The exquisite sensations were almost too much to bear, like a bright light to eyes that had been too long in darkness. A salty tear stung her lips where his assault had left them raw, and her voice was ragged as she struggled to breathe.

But as his hands crept down to explore the hollow at the small of her back, her body softened against his. She might have been made of moonbeams. Her bones were not stiff, her flesh not fixed. She was some magic mixture he alone could concoct—warm, milky, opalescent and bubbling with need.

Her heart, too, softened, as his hands moved across her, easily working their enchantment. One small part of her stood back, amazed to find that she was still capable of such sweet submission, but it was such a small part. The rest of her was sinking willingly into the deep trance of love.

It must have been that part of her that heard, as though from far, far away, the rumble of an engine as a car swung into the long Larkin driveway. Someone was coming home.

A remnant of willpower fluttered within her like the tattered flag of a vanquished country, and she struggled back toward consciousness. She mustn't let her guests see her like this, necking boldly in the woods like a giggling kitchen maid. "Drake, no," she managed.

The spell broke as he released her with a rough snap. He stood abruptly back from her, looking at her with eyes as darkly blue as a stormy sky.

"Why not? You want me." His eyes ran down past her swollen lips to watch the heavy swell of her breathing. "Your good doctor never made you feel like that. You've spent the past six years turning to stone. Dammit, Amanda, you don't just want me. You *need* me."

The image was piercingly apt, and the truth of it took her breath away. That was exactly how she'd felt for six years now—like a stone woman, as cold and bloodless as the sad cupid beside them. And yet with one kiss he had chiseled years of protective stone from her heart and sent the hot blood coursing through her veins with painful speed. She looked away, frightened by the power of her feelings. Need him? Only as much as she needed air and water.

But then he heard the car, too, its tires crunching across gravel as it came closer. His eyes flickered toward the driveway and then back to Amanda. "I see. All right. Not here." He held out his hand. "Come."

She didn't take it, holding tightly to the tree behind her with shaking fingers. Now that he had pulled away, she could finally feel her senses steadying. Her roller-coaster emotions had miraculously slid to a safe stop. She couldn't risk touching him again. It would be tantamount to climbing aboard the roller coaster again, and she knew this time there would be no stopping—not until it crashed to its own fiery demise.

"I don't think so, Drake," she said weakly.

"Why not?" He stared at her for a moment and then dropped his hand slowly. "Oh, I see. Are the Larkins still too good for me?" He let his eyes roam insolently down the gleaming white apron. "I doubt it. You're not the pampered princess of the house anymore, are you, Mandy? In fact, I've heard you Larkins are hanging on to this place with a mortgage and a prayer." He leaned nonchalantly against the nearest tree, his voice contemptuous and his eyes hard. "I'm actually surprised my kisses aren't more welcome now that they're attached to a steady income. It was my understanding your affections always went to the highest bidder."

The smoldering ashes of the passion that had consumed her a moment ago flickered and combusted once more, this time into rage. "You're disgusting!" The words blazed from her, and she gripped the tree so hard her knuckles turned as white as her apron, as she fought the urge to weep. She had already exposed herself too much. She couldn't let him see how fully he had destroyed her hard-won equilibrium. "Do you think I don't see through your act, Drake? You don't want *me*. You just want the thrill of making love to me here, in this house, the house you were thrown out of. You want to prove to yourself that you're better than we are."

"I've known that for years," he inserted disdainfully. "I don't have to prove it."

"I think you do," she insisted. "I think the things my grandmother said really got under your skin. Well, if it makes you happy, I'll be glad to admit you've got more money than the Larkins. You're rich and we aren't, and I'm sure your shiny new Jaguar makes you feel like a man. Bully for you. But we've changed places in another way, too. You see, *you're* the one who's a snob now. You're the one who thinks money is everything." She tugged at her apron. "When you belittle us for having to cook and clean, you drag yourself down to Olivia's level. Which simplifies things considerably for me. Now I can despise you both."

He didn't answer. And moving as firmly as she could on legs that still felt only half-solid, she left him there, alone with the mournful cupid and the cold black pond.

By MIDMORNING the next day Atlanta was gleefully celebrating the arrival of the first snow of the season. Amanda, who sat in mute frustration behind the wheel of the stalled Cadillac, was less thrilled.

A border of snowflakes framed the windshield, giving the scene beyond the sentimentality of a Christmas card. It was the kind of day she usually loved to paint, when the pines seemed to have been dipped in vanilla frosting and the very air danced with white excitement, but today she stared out at the scene grimly, not even noticing its crisp beauty.

Leaving the key dangling uselessly in the ignition, she hooked her elbows in the hollows of the steering wheel and cupped her chin in her gloved hands. Now what? She *had* to get into town this morning. She peered out the rear window, trying to gauge how far she'd come from Mount Larkin before stalling. Maybe three-quarters of a mile?

She twisted her wrist for another look at her watch and then wrenched the key sideways in its slot once again. And again. Nothing. Not even a tentative rumble. She muttered an oath under her breath and thumped the steering wheel with her open palm. By the time she walked back to the house and called the auto club and a taxi, she'd be an hour late for her appointment. And sopping wet. And mad as a hornet.

Still, she had little choice. She gathered up her valise and purse, buttoned the top button of her light gray overcoat and pushed open the door. Instantly the wind attacked her cheeks, and shivering, she flipped up her collar and walked.

As she made her way up the long hill toward home, her thighs already feeling the pull, she framed apologies in her mind. Mr. Tindal required his clients to be as prompt about their appointments as he expected them to be with their payments. She could just imagine the downward pull of his mouth if she told him the car was on the fritz again. She had expected to have bought a new car by now. Maybe not a Cadillac this time but a new Chevy that worked would be far more desirable than a twelve-year-old Cadillac that didn't.

In spite of the snow she saw the Jaguar at the top of the hill long before she heard it. It seemed to stretch and mold itself silently to the curves in the road. Finally its purr became audible, followed by a deep smooth roar as the driver downshifted. The car slowed to a crawl—Drake had seen her, too.

When he got close enough he waved, and for a childish moment of panic she wished she could dart behind one of the snow-laden pines and hide. After what she had discovered last night—that Drake's presence was physically painful to her—she needed all the serenity she could muster for the meeting at the bank.

But she fought the impulse and stood still, watching him approach and fighting down the rush of longing the sight of his fair head sent through her.

"Need a ride?" He had slid the window down and was leaning toward her, his hand on the door, ready to push it open.

She hesitated. She couldn't read his mood. When he hadn't come down for breakfast, she had hoped that he might just plan to steer clear of her for the rest of his visit. That would be the easiest way, she told herself.

"Come on," he urged impatiently. "If I'm going to be here a whole week we might as well be on speaking terms." He held out a hand. "I hereby officially apologize for last night. All that is old business, so let's just forget it, okay? Truce?"

She frowned, looking back up the hill toward the house. A mist of light snow obscured it, and she had to admit she wasn't eager to complete the climb. "I don't know... I really need to call the auto club." She gestured toward the Cadillac, which sat just off the road, looking more like a forlorn beached whale than a car.

"So call them from town," he argued sensibly, shoving the door open. "Hop in. I'm not going to bite you, you know." His blue eyes narrowed. "Or is it something else you're afraid of?"

She blushed. "I'm not afraid of anything," she said firmly, sliding in across the glossy leather seats. It was wonderfully warm in the car, and she unbuttoned her coat. "I just wondered if I should leave the car there that long."

He laughed coldly, looking over his shoulder at the Cadillac as he manipulated the Jaguar smoothly back into gear. "You should leave it there forever!" He subtly increased the speed. "You were being carted around in that car back before I was mowing lawns. I'd say it's about had it."

Though only his profile was visible to her, she could see the now familiar twisted grin, and realized he was still in a sour mood. Amazing, she thought, the way she could read his face, though some of the lines, especially the deep ones beside his mouth, were new. Indignation shot through her. What was funny about having money problems? He'd had a few of his own, way back when.

She pressed her lips together. "Not everyone can have a Jag, Drake. Some of us have to make do with less exotic transportation."

His voice was still tight as he slipped her a sideways glance. "Now don't be spiteful. And here I was, actually considering giving you a tune-up for Christmas."

Anger rose like bile in her throat, but she forced herself to stare straight ahead, keeping her chin level, as the car swept down the hill. "How generous of you, Mr. Stowe," she said. "But as you'll be long gone by Christmas, that's hardly relevant, is it?"

He laughed loudly at that. "Spoken like a true Southern aristocrat. To hell with the carpetbaggers, is that what you're saying?" He reached over and brushed her hair softly back from her shoulders. "Well, suppose you *earned* the money? Would you take it then?"

She edged sharply away from his hand, from those fingers that with one touch could drain away her resistance. She had learned her lesson. If she had any hope of hanging on to her sanity, she had to accept that his arms were dangerous, that letting him touch her would set up a chemical reaction in which one element embraces and eventually absorbs the other. "You disgust me, Drake."

He stroked the side of her neck lightly, sending goose bumps clear up to the top of her head. "I didn't get the impression last night that my touch disgusted you."

She stiffened against his hand, as though she could deny the chemistry with a force of will. "Really? Then you weren't listening, were you? I think I used that exact word," she reminded him, trying to ignore the melting shivers he was sending through her.

The sports car was suddenly too small to hold them both. His spicy masculine scent mingled with the musky odor of leather and suede and filled her nostrils like incense. The heat from his hard arm seeped into her shoulders and neck, as though it sought to fuse their bodies.

"I'm not talking about your words, Mandy," he contradicted her in a low voice. He moved his hand across her shoulders to her right cheek, where he rubbed a soft circle with his fingertips. "I'm talking about what your body was telling me. In fact, I got the impression that somewhere, deep under all that stony cynicism, is the same beautiful girl I used to know.'' His fingers strayed to her ear, grazing tantalizingly along the soft outer ridge. ''A girl who could make love in the woods, with the summer sun dappling her body, and look like a queen.''

As his words sank in, her heart drummed a painful persistent beat, like a steady knocking on a door that didn't want to open.

She shut her eyes and crossed her arms hard against her chest, symbolically locking the door to her emotions. She mustn't ever open it again. Loving Drake six years ago had almost ruined her life, and loving him now would be even more disastrous. Whatever had brought him to Mount Larkin—curiosity, or revenge, or just leftover physical urges—it certainly hadn't been love.

She tried to pull away from the rhythmic motion of his hand, but the chemical elements had already begun their dangerous bonding, and her neck was stiff as steel. She could not move.

Desperately, she gathered her pride around her. ''That girl is gone, Drake,'' she said, her lips stiff and her voice strange, as though she were an animated statue that had been programmed to speak.

He looked at her through narrowed eyes. ''No. She's just lost. I can still find her.''

''You?'' She met his eyes and spoke in a voice low with banked anger. ''You, Drake? You're the one who destroyed her.''

With a low curse he pulled his arm away and clenched the steering wheel with both hands so tightly his gloves stretched to white gold across his knuckles.

Finally released from the hypnotic embrace, she breathed deeply and, getting her bearings slowly, realized that they had come to a stop at a red light within a block of the bank building. She could see, down the street, the huge green wreath that blinked relentlessly over the double doors, beckoning customers in to withdraw money for holiday shopping.

Making a sudden decision, she wrenched the car door open and swung her feet out violently. The blast of cold air was bracing, as effective as a slap in the face for dispelling hysteria.

"This is where I get off," she said, leaning down to make sure he heard her and spacing the words meaningfully. She was glad to see the grin was gone. "For good."

He stared at her for a long moment, his eyes hard, like glittering blue stones. Then he reached a gloved hand to the shift, thrusting it into gear. The muscles in his right leg tensed as he revved the engine, and the car growled impatiently. "We'll see," he bit back. "We'll see."

She slammed the door on the implied threat and without looking back walked briskly toward the bank.

She was relieved to attain the bustling peace of the lobby where Muzak played carols softly and the tellers handed candy canes out to customers' children. She welcomed the need to turn her thoughts away from Drake altogether. She was even thankful when Mr. Tindal's secretary asked her to wait. She needed a chance to get her mind—and her body—under control. She observed with some shame that her hands were still shaking and her knees felt perilously soft. Mr. Tindal and the Vermont Innkeeping executive, knowing nothing of Drake Daniels, would think all the shivery confusion was over the new partnership, and that would never do.

She twisted her watch. Damn Drake Daniels, anyway. She turned the pages of a magazine blindly.

She did so want to impress this stranger, this new investor who waited for her behind Mr. Tindal's oak-paneled doors. She wanted him to trust her, to believe that she was capable of running Mount Larkin without his interference.

He *had* to. The idea of sharing Mount Larkin—even a small part of it—was horrible to her. Oh, she knew they'd had to do it, find money somewhere, and that her lack of ownership—thanks to Olivia—left her no legal say in the matter. But why now, when it felt like home for the first time in her life? Wasn't it ironic? When she had left Mount Larkin six years ago to marry Richard, she had hoped never to see the house again. And when, only three short years later, she had returned, newly a widow with a toddler in hand, she had approached the house with pure dread. Her memories had hardly been happy ones—the lonely childhood under Olivia's domination, the accident; even the memories of the days with Drake were more bitter than sweet.

But Cicely had needed her help, and she and Julie had desperately needed somewhere to live. So out of love for her aunt and out of financial necessity, she had slaved there for the past three years, trying to make Mount Larkin self-supporting. And amazingly, the hard work had done what her coldly privileged childhood had not—it had taught her to love the house. She knew every teardrop crystal in every chandelier, every dusty cluster of grapes in the moldings, every creak in the ancient hardwood floors.

Her grip on the arms of the chair tightened until white crescents formed on her fingernails. What would this indifferent investor want to change? Perhaps he wouldn't like the idea of a little girl chattering at the breakfast table, bothering the guests. Perhaps he'd want Amanda and Julie to live somewhere else. She had no legal rights, after all. Old Olivia had decided to write Amanda out of her will the night she found out about Drake. A sordid affair with a hired hand? Not for the Larkins of Mount Larkin! The house had been left entirely to Cicely, with a provision that it must never be given to Amanda. Why, she could only imagine how much her grandmother would resent even her presence in the house, would detest the fact that Cicely let her virtually run the place.

So this man could ask her to leave. And then someone else would sit on the upstairs porch, tired from spring cleaning, and watch blue jays swing in the magnolias. Would the honeysuckle bloom for them the way it had for her last year? And would other lovers discover the sunny corner where she had given herself to Drake?

And what about Julie? Julie belonged there, Amanda told herself fiercely. She was a Larkin, and she belonged at Mount Larkin. Cicely had already made her own will—with considerably less fanfare than Olivia—and had left everything she owned to

Julie. Julie had always been told that the house was her very own castle.

"Mr. Tindal can see you now." The smiling secretary stood over Amanda.

Amanda dropped her magazine and, still lost in her thoughts, followed the other woman through the carpeted hall to the heavy oak door of the vice-president's office. Mr. Tindal rose politely behind his desk and held out a hand.

It was then that she saw the other man, who sat comfortably cross-legged in an armchair by the big window. His familiar twisted grin revealed how much he was enjoying this, his second cruel surprise.

"Amanda," Mr. Tindal was saying, "I'd like you to meet Drake Daniels."

CHAPTER FIVE

DRAKE DANIELS.

For a moment she was afraid she might laugh.

By all sensible accounts this was where she should weep and wring her hands and curse the fate that had brought him back into her life. But perversely all she felt was an irrational, bubbling geyser of laughter.

Apparently her system had absorbed all the shocks it could handle in one twenty-four hour period, and now it wanted to meet this new problem with an incredulous, embarrassingly inappropriate giggle.

She managed to restrain herself, though, and simply smiled broadly over at Drake as she shook Mr. Tindal's thin cool hand.

"Oh, there's no need to introduce us, Mr. Tindal. Drake Daniels and I know each other quite well. Though I admit there seems to be no end to his little surprises." She extended her hand to Drake, who rose from his chair slowly, a reluctant smile of admiration playing at his lips. "Mr. Vermont Innkeeping, I presume?"

He took her hand in a warm firm grip. "None other."

Mr. Tindal pushed his glasses up on his nose, looking somewhat bewildered. "Well, then!" He turned from one to the other helplessly and dropped onto his leather chair. "Well!"

"Well!" Amanda contributed helpfully, settling onto the soft plaid armchair and feeling the laughter threatening again. It was ludicrous—so utterly absurd.

With raised eyebrows she turned to Drake, who was still smiling, though his eyes were alert. "I had no idea a little revenge was so valuable to you, Drake," she said sweetly. "Frankly we would have upped the price if we'd known it was you."

Turning away before he could answer, she explained to Mr. Tindal confidingly, "You see, Drake hates the Larkins. My family wasn't very nice to him a few years back. He probably would have paid *any* price to get a piece of Mount Larkin."

Mr. Tindal looked stunned and shot Drake an apologetic glance. "Really, Amanda... I don't know exactly why... I don't know what the relationship..." When she didn't respond, he turned stern and glared at her over his cheaters. "I don't think your grandmother would have wanted you to behave this way."

At that Amanda did laugh. She laughed heartily and stood up from her chair.

"Oh, you don't know how wrong you are, Mr. Tindal. But perhaps Drake will fill you in after I'm gone. I think you'll find this is his idea of a joke." She draped her coat over her arm and reached for the doorknob. "But I really haven't time to play any more games with him now. I have a business to run."

She heard Mr. Tindal sputtering as she exited, but she didn't even glance back, feeling certain that

Drake's lips were wearing that infuriating crooked smile of his. The hallway seemed to have stretched to twice its length as she walked down it, refusing to hurry, and by the time she reached the lobby, she discovered she was shaking all over.

She leaned against a holly-garlanded pillar to steady herself. Drake was their long-awaited investor, the man behind the anonymous Vermont Innkeeping Investment Corp. That meant he could . . . She grabbed her elbows to keep her fingers from shaking. Oh, god, what now? Now he could come to Mount Larkin whenever his whimsy suggested it, and she would have no power to make him go. She pressed her trembling lips together and tried to think.

But her mind wouldn't stay still long enough for her to grab at a coherent thought. She squeezed her coat against her chest, wondering stupidly how a person could feel so close to tears and laughter at the same time.

"Here. Drink this." A paper cone of water was thrust in front of her, and she looked up.

Drake was standing beside her, his eyes hard.

She shook her head and turned away. "Go away," she said flatly. Her legs had begun to feel dangerously weak, and she scanned the lobby for an empty chair.

"Drink it," he insisted, taking her limp hand and pressing the cool cup into it. "You need it. You're looking a little white. It's a form of shock."

"Shock?" She spat the word back at him. "Oh, you'd like that, wouldn't you?" She glared at his expressionless, bronzed face and tried to resist the urge to fling the water into it. Maybe that would shock *him*. "You've been trying to reduce me to a helpless mass of jelly ever since you got here, one way or another.'' She dumped the cup, water and all, into a tall brass cigarette stand, and the water seeped slowly into the white sand, turning it a sickly gray. Then she faced him squarely, her jaw tight. ''Well, it's not going to work, Drake. I'm a Larkin, and Larkins don't crumble that easily. It's not shock you see on my face. It's fury. And shame. Shame that I didn't see you for what you were six years ago!''

She flung her coat over her shoulders and, without a backward glance, stalked toward the doors. She had to get away from him. A cab maybe, though she could ill afford it. She'd never be able to think clearly in that Jaguar, with his musty scent filling her nostrils, his shoulder brushing hers with fire, and the engine rumbling beneath her feet, sending tremors of suppressed power up through her body. If only her legs would carry her out into the safely anonymous throng of Christmas shoppers. But anger had made her weak, and it was like trying to run on rubber stilts.

Just by the door he caught her. Without a word he slipped his arm around her shaking shoulders and guided her through the doors.

And then in spite of herself she was glad of his support, as the threat of tears advanced. The urge to laugh had dissipated completely. It wasn't funny—it was a nightmare. What was she going to do? What was she going to tell Cicely? She choked back a sob. Oh, god. What was she going to do?

She noticed almost nothing of her surroundings, except that it was very cold, and Drake's warm arm provided her only protection against the stiff wind that blew at her back.

He didn't try to talk to her, as though aware she couldn't respond, not yet. He just closed his warm palm around her upper arm firmly enough to steer her down the crowded streets.

Gradually her misery subsided. She began to breathe normally, and as her senses cleared she became aware of where she was. Surprised, she saw that they had reached the heart of downtown. The snow was still falling lightly between the tall, gunmetal-blue buildings that obscured the sky. It dusted her eyelashes with sparkling white and melted like tears on her hot cheeks. Metallic Christmas trees dangled from lamp posts, and the tuneless ringing of a Salvation Army bell followed them down the street.

"Where are we going?" she asked quietly, indifferent to her implied capitulation.

"Lunch," he answered calmly and, with slight pressure on her arm, turned her toward a tall building. "You'll feel better when you get something to eat."

The Peachtree Plaza? At the doorway, she hesitated, her eyes narrowing at his concern for her well-being.

"You do need to eat," he said, "and we have a lot to talk over."

She merely nodded and kept walking, ignoring the interior skyscrapers of lighted balconies and waterfalls of plantings. She stopped in front of the tubular glass elevator and waited passively for him to press the button. If he expected her to express pleasure at his choice of restaurants he would be disappointed. Right now anything she ate would taste like cardboard.

In fact, she wondered how she'd be able to eat at all. Her throat was tight and narrow, and just swallowing was painful. She took several deep breaths, and by the time they were seated and Drake ordered a peach daiquiri for her and a straight whiskey for himself, she was feeling marginally composed.

Summoning all her Larkin pride, she gave him a straight look. "Perhaps we'd better get down to business. You have an agenda, I suppose?"

Ignoring her question he unbuttoned his dark jacket and leaned back in his chair, seeming totally at ease in spite of her combative tone.

"Feeling better?" His eyes appraised her, as though gauging her condition.

"I won't feel better until I know what you want," she bit back. She leaned forward, her hair swinging over her shoulders. Its auburn silk flamed against the soft peach tablecloth. "Listen, Drake. I think it's time we stopped playing cat and mouse. Just tell me what your terms are."

The waitress appeared with their drinks and placed them on the table, offering a coy smile to Drake. Amanda concealed her impatience as best she could while Drake gave their food order. Still breathing deeply, she folded her napkin into tiny triangles and watched the city swing slowly beneath them, while her mind raced once again through its set of unanswerable questions. What would she tell Cicely? What would she tell Julie? What would she *do*?

Cicely would be so distressed. It shamed Amanda to think that her own rash actions all those years ago had led to this dilemma. If only she had resisted him then. If only she had been able to stay out of those hard golden arms, none of this would have happened. The room swam into a watery peach blur as tears sprang to her eyes, and she took a quick gulp of the daiquiri. The icy heat slid down her throat easily, clearing the tears away, and she took another swallow.

"Well?" She turned back to Drake, who was now watching her intently. "What are your terms? What do you want?"

Tilting his shot glass, he stared for a long moment into the golden liquid, as though looking for an answer there. When his eyes came back up to hers, they were dark and unreadable.

"Did you ever consider the possibility that I just wanted to help? That I heard you were in financial difficulties and wanted to see what I could do?"

She gave a short bark of laughter. "Never."

"Ahh." He looked straight at her, but his cobalt eyes seemed focused on something far away. "You think you know me that well, do you?"

She sipped at her daiquiri. The alcohol was calming her, and she felt more in control. She gave him a small cold smile. "Let's just say I've met generous people before. My husband, Richard, for instance, was a generous person. You? Well, you don't quite fit the mold."

She saw his hand close hard around his glass, going white at the knuckles, and the reaction sent a rush of bitter pleasure through her. She hurt so horribly inside that she wanted to hurt him in return.

"Oh, yes," he drawled. "The good doctor. He must have been generous of spirit. As I understand it, he didn't have much else with which to exercise generosity."

"Richard was a wonderful man," she defended hotly, realizing too late that he had meant to goad her. Why, she wondered, was he so hateful about Richard? Why did he feel such hostility toward her dead husband, a man he'd never even met? Richard had never done a cruel thing in his too-short life. Too bad one couldn't say the same about Drake.

"Yes, a paragon. So you've said," he murmured, and sipped his drink casually, though his eyes watched her over the rim.

Trying to regain her dignity, Amanda dropped her hands into her lap and spoke swiftly. "That's right. But as I've said, why don't we get down to business? What do you want from us? Why were you willing to invest fifty thousand dollars in an unspectacular little bed-and-breakfast place in Atlanta? I'm sure there are more exotic investments out there for someone with your—" she made the word sound ugly "—assets."

He didn't answer right away, waiting as the waitress served their salads. Then picking up his fork, he returned Amanda's cold smile.

"Maybe I just wanted the right to come and go as I please at Mount Larkin." He speared an olive and ate it, adding, "Through any door I like."

With his eyebrows raised he looked the picture of nonchalance, but something, maybe something just behind the dark blue of his eyes, spoke to her of a deeper emotion.

She picked up her fork but didn't use it. Her gray-green eyes showed open disbelief. "That can't be worth fifty thousand dollars to you, Drake," she said, shaking her head. "Now that you're the glamorous Roger Stowe, doors everywhere are open to you. You don't need ours."

He stared down at his drink and rubbed his thumb thoughtfully across the glass's clear rim. "Perhaps you're right," he said without looking up. "I may have overestimated the worth of that particular pleasure."

He lifted his head suddenly, and the bitterness on his face shocked her. "Though there is no doubt I've enjoyed hearing the story of your idyllic marriage to the incomparable Richard from your own pretty lips."

Amanda caught her breath. With her mind she heard the sarcasm in his voice, but her heart was hearing something else completely, something she faintly recognized but didn't understand. She had heard it in Julie's voice once or twice, when she realized Santa Claus was just an old man in a costume, or when she spied the wire that had made Tinkerbell "fly." It was the sound of the cruel needle of reality pricking the translucent bubble of a dream.

She looked away, unable to face that surprisingly bleak look. What had his dream been, she wondered? What had he hoped to accomplish by returning to Mount Larkin? Whatever it was, she felt certain he'd been disappointed.

A small twist of compassion ran through her, and she marveled that it could exist alongside the fear and fury that filled her. She knew all too well the sadness of dreams that died.

But then, she had heard it said that revenge, though a sweet dish, left a bitter aftertaste. He should have thought of that before he came sneaking back into her life seeking revenge. If his thoughts were bitter now, they were nothing compared to her own.

They ate in silence for a few minutes while she considered the situation. At last, as she mused on his last words, a glimmer of hope flickered in her. Maybe, if Drake really had been disappointed by what he'd found at Mount Larkin, he could be persuaded to give up his vendetta and go away. She gripped her fork hard, trying not to let her budding excitement show. Maybe there was a way out of this quagmire.

If only she had enough money to buy him out! He of all people might be willing to kiss a bad bargain goodbye for the right price.

But immediately her hopes fell. There wasn't enough money—if there had been, she would have been Mount Larkin's benefactor, not Drake Daniels, and all this would never have happened. And if anyone else had been willing to lend them the money... well, they had exhausted every conventional avenue before agreeing to accept an investor. Mount Larkin was already mortgaged to its chimneytops.

When Richard died, he had left Amanda only a small life insurance, and most of that had been used to send Martin to medical school. Amanda planned to give the remainder to him when he finished his residency, to set up a practice, or put toward a house, or something.... She didn't think of the money as hers—hadn't married Richard for money. She had nursed him and cared for him during his last difficult years, but he had more than repaid her. He had worked a miracle in her life, had in fact virtually saved it. He had definitely saved Julie's.

And now there was only twenty thousand dollars left, and Drake had invested fifty. Her money wasn't enough. Unless...

"Another daiquiri?"

Amanda looked up, startled. She hadn't even realized the waitress was back. She waved her hand. "No...no thanks." She didn't want to get fuzzy-minded. If this plan were to work, she'd need all her wits about her.

Drake, too, declined a second drink, and when they were alone again, Amanda cleared her throat and started in before she could lose her nerve. It was a long shot, but it was her only shot.

"Drake," she began tentatively, squeezing her hands together in her lap to steady them.

He raised his dark eyebrows in wry acknowledgement. "Amanda."

She flushed at his sardonic tone. If only he weren't in such a black mood. It might be easier if he were more receptive. But it wasn't ever going to be easy, she reminded herself, so she might as well just jump in.

She swallowed hard. "Drake, I have a proposition to make."

Leaning back in his chair, he rested his square chin on his hand and brushed a long forefinger across his hard upper lip. "Hmm...is that as interesting as it sounds?"

She tilted her head self-consciously and tucked a loose strand of hair behind her ear, annoyed but struggling to conceal her annoyance in the interests of diplomacy. "It might be," she said. "I hope you'll think it is."

He smiled then, but thinly, and he didn't invite her to go on. She felt her courage taking a dive through her stomach. He wasn't going to help. Well, that was typical.

"Here it is, then," she continued staunchly. "I'll tell you how I see this whole thing. I think we have a... common problem. You've made an investment you don't seem to be terribly happy with—I don't blame you for that. Mount Larkin is just a small place, and we're not doing all that well yet."

"I'm not sure that can't be remedied," he said in a reasonable tone. "I may just stay a while and see if I can't make Mount Larkin's business pick up. I may need to study the situation and recommend some changes."

Stay? Oh, no! Her heart galloped crazily. Last night in the garden, she had managed to say no to her rioting senses and pull herself out of his arms. But that one brief struggle had left her limp. How many more nights would she be able to say no—to deny his obvious physical desire as well as her own deep needs? A week, a month perhaps? She looked at him now, and a current of panicked need traced through her. No, not that long. Even a few more hours might be fatal.

His eyes gleamed with an unholy amusement, and she squirmed, wondering if he knew what she was thinking. A smile played at his lips as he watched her, and she felt uncomfortably like a butterfly pinned to a board. But she had to go on. She had no choice.

"Well, that's not all. To be honest with you, my aunt won't be exactly comfortable with the idea of having you for a partner." She smiled placatingly, hoping to take the sting out of the words. "She's always been a little intimidated by you—you've noticed that, surely. And I don't think you and I would do very well as partners, either—do you?''

He shook his head slowly. "Probably not. Our track record is very poor so far.''

"Well, then,'' she said, speaking more quickly now that she was approaching her point, "here's my proposal. I have a little money left from Richard's life insurance. Not much—only about twenty thousand dollars. It's not enough, I know, to buy out your partnership. But I was thinking that perhaps it would be enough to... Well, if you still maintained the partnership on paper, and still received your share of any profits, then maybe you'd rather just go on back to writing your books...and you wouldn't need to bother with us and the house and—''

She stopped suddenly, flushing. It sounded so horrible this way, so clearly an attempt to buy him off. She felt degraded by even having uttered the words. And yet... And yet, what else could she do? She just couldn't let him stay. She studied her forgotten salad intently, unable to look him in the eye.

"I know it's not much,'' she repeated miserably, "but it's all I have. I could try to save more to give you later....''

She looked up finally, sensing that he had gone ominously still. She tried desperately to read his expression, but it was a perfect blank. The only telling signs were the deepened lines along his mouth and the frozen stillness of his body.

"Drake?'' She rested the palms of her hands on the tablecloth. "Will you consider it?''

He didn't answer her for a long cold moment. And when he finally did, his voice was low and even, but there was a dangerous edge to it.

"Let me make certain I've understood you," he said slowly. "You're willing to *give* me twenty thousand dollars, everything you have in the world, if I'll get out of your life and stay out?"

"I didn't mean it to sound like that," she began, stumbling. "Y-you're making it sound much worse—"

"No, I'm just cutting through that ridiculous smoke screen of words. Did you know, Amanda, that when you're nervous you chatter?" He abandoned his pose of nonchalance and leaned forward.

She pulled back instinctively. His bronzed fingers resting lightly on the peach-colored cloth were oddly threatening.

"But don't worry. I heard what you were really saying—just as I heard what your grandmother was saying six years ago when she made a similar offer. You're not nearly as smooth as she was, you know. She wasn't nervous at all. She came right to the point. There's a certain dignity in that. It's honest, at least."

She felt her face growing red, as though he had slapped her. He dared to speak of dignity, of honesty! Well, he'd see that she was his match any day. She pulled out her checkbook holder and placed it on the table. Slipping the matching pen out of its leather ring she clicked the point open with a sharp jab and carefully wrote out a check for twenty thousand dollars. She refused to allow her hand to waver, and the Amanda Larkin Hamilton signature was dark and bold.

"All right, Drake." She tore the check slowly from the book and struggled to keep the betraying tremble out of both her voice and her hands. "By all means, let's get right to the point. I do want you out of my life. If I had twenty *million* dollars, I'd use it to get rid of you. Will you take it or not?"

He didn't answer, didn't even look at the check, and frustrated, she ground her fists on the table. "You said yourself it wasn't as much fun tormenting the poor Larkins as you had anticipated." She pushed the check toward him. "Go on, Drake. Why don't you just take the money and run? Go back to your world of Jaguars and groupies and royalty checks. You don't need us—and we don't want you."

She leaned back, spent. "Is that clear enough?"

Wrapped up in her fiery indignation, she hadn't noticed until now how frightening he looked. His eyes were almost black, and his jaw was set at a grim angle. His hands were now clenched and his body was poised and rigid.

"Quite clear enough," he said, and his voice was like his body, tight and poised for battle. "Congratulations, Amanda. Your grandmother would be proud."

Still ignoring the blue rectangle that lay on the table between them, he beckoned to the waitress with an air of such unassailable authority that she came scurrying from across the room. "The bill," he said, and the woman hurried away to get it, all smiles forgotten.

Amanda forced herself to remain calm. "Then may I have an answer, please?"

His dark eyes impaled her. "Patience, Amanda. It's the most important asset in business. Even more important than cash."

"But—"

"I've paid in advance for a week at the lovely Mount Larkin," he said, interrupting her frantic words with his lazy drawl. "That means I have until next Sunday morning to make up my mind. I'll think over your generous offer. And I'll tell you before Sunday morning what my answer is."

She frowned, dismayed. She had foolishly hoped that he would leave right away. A whole week—lying in her old bed, with her knowing he slept just down the hall. Watching his impassive face and longing for a more tender expression, but knowing his glorious smile could only torture her with dreams of what might have been. Listening to him laugh, with Lina perhaps, a deep low chuckle that would vibrate down her spine, and knowing they'd never share another night of such intimate laughter. A whole week. She felt light-headed, and took a deep breath.

Even if *she* could endure his presence, how would Cicely stand up under the strain? She couldn't. And Cicely mustn't know that Drake was their investor, at least not until Amanda could tell her he was gone for good. Was that possible? Would he be willing to keep this whole mess a secret, or would he be too eager to watch another Larkin squirm?

She bit her lip, holding back the urge to beg. How he would love to see her beg!

He still hadn't so much as glanced at the check. He obviously wasn't going to. With an awkward motion of retreat she slid it back across the table and fingered it nervously.

"Can we keep this just between us until then?" She presented her request as evenly as she could. "I'd rather my aunt knew nothing of this until it's resolved."

"Just between us? How charming." His strong lips curled in a mockery of a smile. "Our little secret. It will be just like old times."

His sarcasm was like the slow drag of a knife through the paper-thin control in which she'd wrapped herself. When had he developed such a sharp edge, such a fine blade of cruelty?

But if she bled, she refused to gratify his ego by letting him see the wound.

"Fine," she said coolly, though her heart was burning in her chest. She held up the check briefly before slipping it into the deep pocket of her dress. "And remember—any time you want it, this is waiting for you."

CHAPTER SIX

"I OUGHT to whack it all off," Amanda grumbled, watching impatiently in the mirror as her aunt painstakingly French-braided her long, auburn hair. "At the ears."

Cicely tsked dismissively and pushed Amanda's head forward, the better to reach the last silky segments of hair.

"I should," Amanda muttered defiantly into her lap. "I'm too busy to go through this every Saturday night. Besides I'm too old to wear my hair halfway down my back."

"You're not acting like it," her aunt said, humphing slightly as she stretched to reach a green silk ribbon that lay on the edge of the dresser. She threaded it into the braid. "You're acting Julie's age. Sit still. What is wrong with you tonight, anyway? You know your hair looks wonderful like this. Remember what that young man said—the one who stayed a couple of nights last summer?"

Amanda shrugged. She remembered. He hadn't been the first male guest to admire the way the curling tip of the braid fell between her shoulder blades, which had been exposed by the scooped back of her party dress. He'd just been the most poetic. And the most persistent.

"If it would keep guys like that from pestering me, I'd cut it in a minute," she grumbled. "I understand that men have an obsession about long hair, but we don't have to cater to their every fetish, do we?"

As though she sensed that Amanda's words were just irritable rumblings of a stormy mood, Cicely didn't bother to respond. Grumpy and restless, Amanda stared down at the gaily colored plaid taffeta skirt she knew so well. She never wore it without remembering... Perhaps she should change. But she didn't have many party dresses now, and she had worn this one to dozens of Saturday night dinners. She plucked absently at a loose thread, her thoughts racing back through the years to a night six years ago, when the dress had been brand new....

She had been to a fraternity dance—she couldn't remember her escort's name now, or what Greek letters had hung over the door. Even the dance itself hadn't been terribly memorable—just another pretty kaleidoscope of pink chiffon, yellow lanterns and purple sky designed to amuse rich boys and girls. But after the dance a group of kids had stopped at the University Center for coffee. She almost hadn't joined them. It had been late, and she'd been tired. She often wondered how her life would have turned out if she had gone straight home, or if Drake had left a few minutes earlier.

But she didn't go home, and he was there when she and her friends arrived. He was alone, sitting in a shadowy corner of the UC, bent over a textbook. Even so, she couldn't help noticing him—obviously several years older...an air of mystery...too handsome to be alone. One of the "chiffon girls" had been particularly blatant in her interest, admiring his broad muscular back with tipsy arrogance.

For a moment Amanda had giggled along with the others. But then Drake had looked up at them, and she'd felt suddenly ashamed. Her eyes dropped before his sardonic blue gaze, and she winced for the other girl's continued coquetry. Somehow Amanda hadn't been surprised when, ignoring the flagrant invitation, Drake had folded his book and left.

Amanda never attended another fraternity party. It was crazy, she knew, but the brief look into Drake's deep blue eyes had soured her on girls who never stopped laughing and callow boys who talked in football metaphors and compared hangovers during English 101.

But no matter how often she lingered hopefully at the UC she never saw Drake there again. He might have been only a figment of her restless imagination. Finally she gave up and agreed, much to her grandmother's delight, to go out with one of the stockbrokers engaged in handling the family's investments. He wasn't her mystery man, but at least he was older, like Drake, and had a sheen of success that passed for glamour.

Pleased with the match, Olivia showed Amanda more affection during those months than ever before, and Amanda's heart, accustomed to starvation rations, sought such warmth. And tragically, she mistook the display for love—so she let the stockbroker keep calling.

The night Amanda showed her grandmother the sparkling diamond engagement ring, Olivia was ecstatic. She even, unprecedentedly, embraced Amanda and kissed her on the head. For a while, basking in the glow of her grandmother's approval, Amanda had been happy, and had almost managed to ignore her own nagging doubts.

Almost. But then, one early summer morning, she'd run into a very tall, very bronzed worker in the back gardens of Mount Larkin, and this time his cobalt-blue eyes had been smiling....

"All done!" Cicely was holding out her hand, and Amanda rose slowly, in a way relieved that her reminiscing was interrupted. It was better not to take the memory any further, into the hot summer months.

Amanda twisted to look in the mirror at her aunt's handiwork. Cicely had outdone herself. The green ribbon was slipped artfully in and out the glossy French braid.

"Thanks, Cicely," she said, trying to make amends for her earlier ill humor. "It looks nice."

"Nice? You look gorgeous, Mandy," Cicely said, fussing proudly at the neckline of Amanda's fitted black bodice. She twirled her niece around and fidgeted with the black satin bow that rode like a bustle on the back of the waistline. "You've always looked beautiful in that dress. If only Drake... I wish you— I wish he—"

"No, you don't." Amanda stopped her with a firm tone. "And neither do I."

Her aunt's eyes clouded and Amanda knew her curtness had hurt her. "Cicely," Amanda said firmly but more gently, "he's leaving tomorrow. Don't get any ideas."

Cicely sighed. "All right, honey," she said regretfully. "But it's hard not to." She peered into the mirror to brush at her own soft gray curls. "When he came, I was honestly afraid. But he's been so nice, don't you think? He's turned into such a nice young man. I just can't help thinking... Maybe you should talk to him about—"

"Stop it." Amanda held her hands palms forward, brooking no more discussion. "He's leaving tomorrow and that's it. Don't get too used to having his help. And don't for one minute imagine I'm going to talk to him about anything. He's leaving tomorrow."

He *was* leaving, wasn't he? She breathed deeply, thinking of the check—he *had* to take it.

But if he was planning to leave, why had he spent all week running around being helpful and charming? When she went to take the garbage out, Drake had already done it. When she checked on the firewood, he smiled and said, "Tom and I did that this morning. You've got enough now to last you the winter." When she climbed the curving stairs, arms loaded with clean linens, she almost stumbled over him, nailing down the loose carpet.

Given the way he felt about her, and about Mount Larkin, it didn't make any sense. It was enough to drive her crazy.

Yesterday, when she had found him rehanging the back gate, it was finally more than she could stand. "What do you think you're doing?" she had blurted, her arms folded angrily.

He had given her a look of such calculated innocence she'd wanted to slap him. "Why, I'm hanging the gate for you, Miss Amanda. Was there something else you needed me to do?"

It was the keenest parody of a bobbing servant. If he'd had a cap, he would have tipped it. Her face burned as she answered him. "You know what I need you to do, Drake. I need you to take my offer and leave."

"But it's only Friday," he had answered smoothly, straightening up to his imposing height and stepping back into his own character. "And until Sunday I'll do as I please."

The nights were even worse. They all sat together in the living room, with the fire crackling and the music rippling through the air. Cicely darned clothes and Amanda fiddled with her sketchbook. Drake played chess with Webster or read poetry with Lina. They might have been one big happy family, and the cozy intimacy was so seductive she had to struggle constantly not to give in to the desire to smile over at him or touch his gleaming head as she passed. Even her fingers betrayed her, and more than once she found his face staring at her from the sketchbook in her lap.

On those nights, she'd close her pad violently and excuse herself, pleading exhaustion. And then she'd collapse into bed and try desperately to fall asleep before she heard his tread on the stairs.

But each night, sleep stubbornly eluded her, and as he passed her door on the way to his room she found herself listening, her heart pounding foolishly in her ears. But he never slowed his pace even fractionally, to acknowledge any awareness of her, and as his steps faded away she turned into her pillow, trying to smother her irrational disappointment.

Well, tomorrow, thank goodness, he would have to answer her, and the charade would finally be over. She would, somehow, make him take the money.

She fluffed out her billowy taffeta skirt with determined bravado and smiled at her aunt.

"Well, how about a smile?" She offered her own brave one as an example. "This is a special night. It's almost Christmas. We're going to trim the tree. Julie will be home soon. We've got a lot to be happy about."

A pink as delicate as the cotton dress Cicely wore crept across her thin cheeks.

"Yes, I guess we do," the older woman agreed throatily, and Amanda knew her aunt had dreams of her own that might come true this Christmas. She recalled the small box Webster had wrapped.

"Go get dressed, then," Amanda ordered affectionately. "You can't spend all your time fixing me up. You've got to look your best tonight, too. I'll go get things ready."

Once downstairs, though, she found that the maid had put everything in order already, and there was nothing for her to do. The unopened boxes of Christmas ornaments stood stacked and waiting in one corner of the large room, and through the doorway she could see the festive table as Maria, their once-a-week maid, laid green-and-gold china against the snowy white cloth. Amanda prowled the room restlessly, trying not to wonder whether Drake would come for dinner.

She tried reading three different books, but the words jumped around on the pages and she gave up. She even phoned Martin, hoping to catch Julie before she went to bed, but there was no answer. Another long day at Disney World, no doubt.

She sighed. How she missed Julie and her easy chatter. Sighing, Amanda knelt on the carpet next to the tall bookcase and pulled out the big black folder in which she kept her sketches of her daughter.

As the book fell open, Julie's bright smile met her gaze, and Amanda smoothed her fingers over the chalk image of golden curls. Her adored daughter. She tried to focus on her, but perversely, even Julie seemed a million miles away right now. Tonight, it seemed, only Drake Daniels's sardonic face would stay before her eyes.

She closed the folder slowly and put it on the coffee table. There was another portfolio, one she hadn't looked at since she had folded it away six years ago. She had vowed never to open it again. But tonight, with loneliness muffling the voice of common sense, she knew she finally wanted to. She reached down, feeling her way through the other books. When her probing fingers encountered the dusty leather, she pulled the portfolio out and, before she could have second thoughts, flung it open.

Pictures scattered, splashing sunlight gold and cobalt blue across the thick green carpet, and Amanda sank weakly back on her heels before the onslaught of memories. Pandora's box couldn't have released more misery than this simple folder.

She picked up a sketch with trembling fingers. Oh, god. Oh, Drake. She had been right to bury these pictures—the pain of seeing them again was almost unendurable.

It wasn't just that Drake's sensuality was palpable, even in a drawing—he still possessed the same enormous sex appeal, the same rugged good looks, the laughing blue eyes, the wide full mouth, the strong bronze fingers.

No, it was something else. It was the ghost of her dreams that had escaped from this portfolio tonight, and it was pressing now against her swollen heart until she felt it might burst. The drawings, amateurish as they were, captured the essence of a young girl's fantasy. The love pictured in his eyes, the tender promise on his lips, the safety his capable hands offered—those were the things that lived on in memory, the things that could never be again, if indeed they'd ever been more than just figments of her deluded dreams.

She crumpled the nearest sketch against her aching chest to fight the growing pain, and bowed her head as the tears filled her eyes.

"Saying your prayers?"

Startled, Amanda looked over her shoulder. Drake stood in the doorway, a twisted smile on his face as he watched her kneeling beside the bookcase. His tone was cutting and, since she didn't trust her voice, she didn't answer him. She turned back to the portfolio and rapidly blinked the tears away while she shoveled the pictures into their case. She flipped it shut, her haste raising a small puff of dust.

Knowing he still stood there, she pushed the portfolio back into the bookcase as calmly as she could and then gathered up the sketches of Julie. Why had he appeared like this, as though he were one of the ghosts she had released?

"Asking for divine intervention in my decision, perhaps?"

Insolence, as usual. The contemptuous tone was like a cold splash on her grief. She snapped shut the second folder.

"I hardly think divine intervention will be necessary," she said coldly, getting to her feet. "I suspect you'll jump at the deal. It's twice what you were offered last time, after all, and pretty good pay for a week's work." She stared at him, her chin lifted. "And now I need to speak to the maid. If you'll excuse me..." She brushed past his tall body, ignoring the black look that settled on his handsome face.

For the next half hour Amanda dawdled in the kitchen, carving extra carrot flowers and polishing a silver pitcher they had no plans to use. She ignored the quizzical looks the hired maid shot her way and kept up a stream of frivolous chatter until she heard voices in the living room.

She arranged her face carefully, promising herself she would enter the living room smiling. A valiant effort, but a swift survey of the room showed her the entrance had been wasted. Drake was not there.

Lina was, though, looking stunning in a skintight metallic blue dress. And so were Tom and Webster, both crisply handsome in tuxedos. They hurried forward to greet and admire Amanda and Cicely, who appeared from the foyer at the same moment.

The conversation flowed comfortably, as it does when friendly people come together. Tender strains of Chopin wafted around the edges of the room, and the spicy scent of the Christmas tree perfumed the air. Someone handed Amanda a cool glass of champagne, and through the open dining-room door she saw the flicker of candlelight against crystal as Maria put the final touches on the table.

It was Mount Larkin as it used to be, Mount Larkin as it ought to be. She should be happy. She shouldn't waste a minute of her special evening, the one evening of the week she didn't have to slave over preparations and clean up herself. But she couldn't relax. She found herself sipping too often at the champagne and listening for the sound of the front door. Would he come back? Or had her last line been too much, finally, for him to stand? She flushed as she remembered what she'd said. It had been terribly belligerent, and she wondered whether it might have been unwise. She had been so careful all week not to antagonize him. She bit her lower lip, and looked toward the door again.

As usual it was Lina who came out with the question.

"Hey—isn't Drake coming?" She pointed accusingly at the empty place setting as they drifted into the dining room and took their seats. "He can't miss dinner tonight!"

Everyone expressed ignorance of Drake's plans, including the hired maid, who met Amanda's inquiring glance with a small shake of her head. So he hadn't even left word with the kitchen, Amanda thought scornfully. Barnyard manners.

Lina frowned, as though she had encountered a perplexing mystery. "I was telling him just this morning how wonderful your Saturday night dinner is, how it's four courses and finger bowls and everything. I told him he might be able to use it in a book sometime. He said it sounded 'absolutely antebellum.' I was just sure he'd come.''

Amanda pressed her lips together. His comment would have indicated just the opposite to her. But Lina didn't know how much Drake had despised Olivia's grand-dame affectations.

Antebellum indeed! Well, now that he owned part of Mount Larkin, he knew how much they had to pay the women who came in from downtown to serve Saturday night dinner. Hardly slave wages! Annoyed, she shook her napkin out of its intricate folds and swept it onto her lap.

"Well," she replied dryly, "since his novels are set in Texas bars and cattle ranches, I don't know how useful he'd find teatime at Tara."

Webster was looking intently at her. Did she sound so bitter? With effort she toned down her voice. "At any rate it appears he's decided to pass up the opportunity," she added smoothly. "We'll leave his setting—" she nodded to the maid, who was standing uncertainly by the unused plate. "But we'll go ahead and get started."

"Nonetheless, he's missing a very special evening," Webster said gallantly as they all started on the crab soup. He caught Amanda's eye, this time with a supportive wink. "I don't know whether it would make a good scene in a Texas murder mystery, but it's a pleasure I always look forward to."

Cicely murmured a grateful thanks and bent modestly over her soup.

"It *does* make good literary material," Lina insisted. "I've written two poems about the Old South already, and both of them were inspired by these dinners.''

"No," Tom Wyndham disagreed as he spooned up the steaming broth. "It's too civilized here, you know? His books are more—I don't know—untamed. There's not enough raw passion here.''

Everyone grinned except Lina. "I thought you said you hadn't read his books," she objected irritably.

"I just did, this week," he retorted, oblivious to Lina's pique, "and were you ever right. They're terrific! And those love scenes really sizzle, don't they, Web?''

"Well, if you think there's no material for raw passion here, you're just blind, Tom, that's all I can say." Lina pouted, stirring her soup vigorously. "Luckily Drake isn't.''

Amanda caught her aunt's worried look and shook her head reassuringly. But she wished she could feel as confident as she appeared. Drake had spent a lot of time with Lina this week, and she was looking rather smug. Amanda suddenly wasn't hungry anymore.

With an effort she smiled at Tom and patted his arm. "I forgive you," she teased gently. "I'm not sure raw passion would be all that comfortable as a way of life, anyway. I think 'civilized' is compliment enough for anybody.''

Luckily the conversation meandered into other streams as the maid took away the soup bowls. Drake's name wasn't mentioned again.

Until he appeared about two hours later.

"White Christmas" had replaced Chopin on the stereo, and Amanda was perched on a tall wooden ladder, carefully arranging glittering silver and gold ornaments on the highest branches of the beautiful tree. Tom stood beneath her, steadying the ladder with one foot and handing her the shining balls as she needed them. Lina was sorting through the Christmas albums, deciding which one to play next, and Webster and Cicely were sitting on the wide sofa, lost in quiet conversation.

Amanda saw Drake's tall figure in the front hall before anyone else did, and for just a moment she felt her balance wobble. She slipped the hook of an ornament onto a branch at random, abandoning her grand design, and grabbed hold of the narrow seat of the ladder to steady herself.

At first he didn't seem to see her. He just stood in the hallway, under the bright circle of light from the chandelier, and stared into the living room at the cozy domestic scene. He obviously had never planned to join their gala evening. He was still casually dressed in boots and blue jeans and a green-and-blue plaid flannel shirt.

Finally his eyes went to the tree and from there up to the top of the ladder where she sat. His expression didn't even flicker with recognition, but their gazes locked. A tingle shivered through her upper body. It felt so much like that first time, when she had sat in this same dress, in the middle of a laughing party, and seen only his eyes across the room.

"Drake! I knew you'd come!" Lina scattered the albums on the floor and leapt to her feet. "Come on in and help, you skunk! We've been waiting for you all night."

Amanda said nothing and didn't move at all. She wasn't sure she could. She might have been one of the shining fragile ornaments that had been hung high, to avoid its getting jostled and broken. But Tom and Webster and Cicely all added their voices to Lina's pleas. "Come on in."

And so he did, though he moved slowly, almost reluctantly into the the room.

"Don't let me interrupt you," he said cordially. "I was just going to apologize for missing dinner. I had another appointment."

"You're not interrupting, silly," Lina insisted, linking her arm through his and pulling him farther into the room. "And you weren't going to try to sneak away without giving me that critique of my poetry you promised, were you?"

Amanda gripped harder at the plank of the ladder. So he had been helping Lina with her poetry, after all—at least in the literal sense.

Cicely was shaking her head reproachfully at Lina. "Now, Lina, you mustn't pester him while he's here. People go on vacation to get a rest from their work." She looked over at Drake with an apologetic smile. "I'm sorry, Drake. Carolina is just so enthusiastic about her poetry—but I'm sure she didn't mean to put you on the spot."

Cicely's easy tone surprised Amanda. She couldn't remember her aunt ever sounding so confident, so much in charge of herself, in front of anyone as intimidating as Drake. Gazing down curiously, Amanda noticed that her aunt's hand was firmly held in Webster's big paw. Suddenly it made sense, in a way. Webster had given her aunt this new strength. Love— real love—could do that.

"Don't worry, Cicely," Drake was answering with a smile of his own. "I've enjoyed reading Lina's poetry. In fact," he said, turning to the girl on his arm, "I've already put the poems back on your desk, Lina, with my notes on top."

Lina squealed and stood on her toes. "I'm too excited to wait until I go to bed to find out. You have to tell me now whether you liked them or not."

Drake patted her arm. "Of course I liked them," he said. "How could anyone help liking such passion? You love the world, Carolina. Your poems are alive with love."

Lina laughed with delight, and she seemed, under his praise, to sparkle all over. "Oh, if I die right here and now, I die happy," she said, hugging his arm. Amanda wouldn't have been surprised to see her kiss his fingers next. How he must love this adulation!

"And such praise coming from you!" Lina gazed up at him with melting blue eyes. "Everybody knows that you're the absolute expert on love! Even Tom said so, just tonight."

But suddenly Drake was shaking his head, his tolerant smile replaced by something darker.

"Don't kid yourself, Lina. I'm no expert on love," he said, and Amanda, who remembered all the subtle changes in his moods, watched a muscle flicking in his strong jaw and knew he was angry. At Lina?

"And neither are my characters. Good Lord, haven't you noticed? They don't have a real love affair. He doesn't even know who she is, really."

He pulled away from her clinging arm and headed for the liquor cabinet, leaving her looking slightly lost behind him. Everyone was awkwardly silent, embarrassed by his outburst.

"No," he said firmly, as he scraped the stopper out of the decanter and poured himself a Scotch. "They don't have love. They have only need and a kind of driven desire. Maybe I'm an expert on those things, but I don't know a damn thing, Lina, about the kind of love you write about—honest, innocent, happily-ever-after love."

He drained half the amber liquid from his tumbler in one fierce swallow. It seemed to help. The muscle in his jaw subsided, and looking calmer, he crooked his finger at Lina.

"Come here," he said more gently. She came obediently forward, and he took her hand in his, patting it as though to smooth away the confusion. "Listen to Uncle Drake, now. My best advice is to forget about the things you read in books like mine. Go home. Find that fellow you write about, the one with the 'too-brown' eyes. Keep writing about how much you love sunsets and sunrises and summer afternoons."

He chucked her chin playfully. "And most importantly don't ever, ever get old and cynical like me."

Finally Lina smiled tremulously. "Okay," she murmured. "I think you're wrong about your books." She ducked her head sheepishly. "But I think I know what you mean."

They all did. Amanda had to admit that it had been neatly and humanely done. Drake Daniels had just told his adoring young ingenue that he wasn't going to take advantage of her, that she should go home to the boys her age and quit pining after him.

Amanda was so very grateful. It was the nicest thing he could have done for Lina, who was, for all her strutting, a sweet girl. But more importantly she was relieved to know he was above such cheap exploitation, that he didn't have to sleep with every pretty girl who threw herself at him.

Even so, she couldn't help feeling sorry for Lina. She knew all too well how difficult it could be to forget Drake Daniels. The poor girl was still looking a little shell-shocked. Amanda tried to think of a way to change the subject.

"Would someone please hand me the angel for the top?" she called down quickly. "Once she's on, I can come down. The air's getting a little thin up here."

Drake looked up from his Scotch, as though he had not seen her there. "Oh, Amanda, is that you? And all this time I thought you *were* the Christmas angel."

Everyone laughed heartily, glad of the diversion. Even Lina looked grateful—and no wonder. Who enjoyed being rejected in public, however gently it was done?

But Drake's laughter seemed forced, especially after his bitterness of just moments before. Quite a mood swing. Amanda wondered whether he might have been drinking before he came back to Mount Larkin. But she was hardly in a position to be critical, she admitted ruefully. Her own champagne glass had been refilled so many times tonight she had completely lost count. Four, maybe? Too many, anyhow, if her easy descents into dizzy awareness of Drake were any measure.

Still chuckling, everyone sifted through tissue and boxes, searching for the gold papier-mâché angel.

Drake finally found her tucked away in a small box by the fireplace and displayed her with a triumphant flourish.

"Voilà!" He crossed to the ladder and held the figure up toward Amanda. "One more angel, coming up."

Amanda bent to take the ornament and saw, as though through a telescope, that gold glitter from the angel's wings had rubbed off on Drake's long bronze fingers. Her own fingers were shaking as they stretched farther and farther toward them.

And then their hands met.

"Amanda," he breathed, and their fingers wound convulsively together, crushing the hapless angel between their palms.

Their eyes met, too, and amazingly his were blazing with the desire she had seen there so many times, so long ago. Dazed by their blue light, she clung to his hard hand. For a hot tingling instant her blood seemed to be made of gold sparks that sped through her veins and exploded around her heart like fireworks.

As quickly as it happened, it was over. Drake was stepping calmly away from the ladder making a show of surveying the decorations, and like a well-oiled robot she was fixing the blandly smiling angel to the tree's peak. If it had not been for the subtle sprinkling of gold glitter in the warm hollows between her fingers, she would have believed she had imagined the whole thing.

"Okay, come on down," Webster called out. "We've got a toast to drink before we can turn on the lights, and Cicely has some exciting news to tell you."

Drake was back on the other side of the room already, talking to Lina. It was Tom who hurried forward to help Amanda down off the ladder. She forced an eager smile onto her face, anticipating her aunt's news.

She had expected to feel so happy at this moment, so thrilled that Webster and her aunt were going to announce their engagement. Instead she felt hopelessly numb and cold, as if when Drake had withdrawn his hand he had smothered the golden sparks forever.

But she mustn't spoil her aunt's special moment. She took a gulp of the champagne Webster handed her—Dutch courage was better than none.

"Don't keep us waiting," she teased as she took her place next to her aunt. "We're dying to hear."

"All right, then." Cicely took Webster's hand and smiled at Amanda. "It's really a Christmas present to Mandy. You've all seen how hard Mandy works around here. Too hard." A chorus of ascent hummed through the room, and Cicely continued, "Well, you should see her when Julie's home—polishing silver and cooking meals and tending to a five-year-old. It's just too much. So starting at the first of the year we're going to hire a full-time maid."

Amanda halted her champagne glass halfway to her mouth. What? She must have had more to drink than she realized. Cicely wasn't making any sense at all.

She stared at her aunt. "Cicely, what do you mean? You know we can't afford to do that. Don't even think about such an extravagance. I can handle the work."

Her aunt was beaming. "That's the rest of the surprise. The cost will be covered by Vermont Innkeeping. I had a call from Mr. Tindal today. He said they think it will be good for business.''

She turned to Amanda, her arms outstretched. ''Isn't it wonderful? Oh, I'm so glad we decided to take their offer!''

CHAPTER SEVEN

AMANDA LOOKED around helplessly. Everyone else seemed jubilant. Tom was congratulating Cicely, and Drake was uncorking another bottle of champagne. She tried to catch his glance, but he carefully avoided making eye contact. Finally Webster handed them each a glass. "A toast," he called out, raising his glass high.

The others did the same, smiling expectantly.

"To Mount Larkin," he said, "and to the two beautiful women who have made it the special house it is. May all three of them prosper!"

Everyone called out enthusiastic agreement, and crystal glasses winked under the sparkling chandelier as they sipped the bubbling liquid.

"Well, I have an announcement, too," Tom chimed in eagerly. "I've been waiting for the perfect moment, and as this seems to be Amanda's night for pleasant surprises, I think I'll add mine now."

Amanda turned toward him, smiling. She hoped, though, that he didn't plan to make his announcement in the form of a toast. The champagne and the startling news had made her fuzzy-minded enough already. "More good news?" she queried.

"Great news," he corrected emphatically and cleared his throat to make a formal announcement.

"I'm here to tell you that the owner of the Southern Galleries has decided to display the work of our own Amanda Larkin in his downtown gallery. Not only that, he wants to buy one of her drawings himself."

Amanda could hardly believe her ears. "Really?" she asked, incredulous. "He liked them that much?"

"Loved them," Tom said smugly. "I told you he would. You're really good, Amanda."

Laughing delightedly, Cicely hugged her. "Oh, Mandy, that's just wonderful."

Lina came up, too, and squeezed her hand. "What a great night for you, Amanda," she said, her voice touched by wistfulness, and Amanda was reminded of the younger girl's earlier disappointment.

"Thanks, Lina," she said, returning the pressure warmly. "You know, it's really been a good night for you, too," she added. "Drake certainly had positive things to say about your poems. And he's quite an authority on writing, you know, even if he's not one on love. You should be very encouraged."

"I know. I am." But Lina spoke dispiritedly, and her blue eyes drifted toward Drake, who was leaning against the mantel, looking utterly marvelous in his faded blue jeans. "It's funny how some men don't even need to get dressed up, isn't it?" She sighed. "Ed—that's the guy back home—sure doesn't look like that in blue jeans."

Amanda chuckled. "Not many men do," she admitted. "But it isn't how they look in jeans that really counts, is it? I'll bet Ed treats you like a princess."

A smile tugged at one corner of Lina's pretty mouth. "Yeah," she said slowly. "Yeah, he does, actually." Her face lost some of its dejection, and she turned twinkling blue eyes back to Amanda. "Besides, I'm not sure I want to go out with a guy who's got eyes more beautiful than mine!"

They both laughed at that, and Amanda reached out to ruffle the younger girl's hair. "Amen!" she agreed heartily.

Amanda made her way back to Tom. "I can't thank you enough," she said. "I still can't believe I've actually sold a picture. Which one did he buy?"

"The one of the dogwood tree. I thought that was your best, too," Tom said, "except for the ones of Julie, but you didn't send any of those. I told him I'd try to talk you into getting some together for hanging. He's really excited about it."

Drake appeared at her elbow suddenly and held up his glass.

"A toast, then, to the man's good taste," he said smoothly, and Amanda, who hadn't realized he was anywhere near enough to hear her conversation, wasn't sure whether or not it was irony she heard in his voice.

"Thank you," she said politely, still trying to meet his eyes, and sipped again with the others. Unfortunately when the toast was over Tom began chattering immediately, and Drake moved away.

"You just have to get together some pictures of Julie," Tom was saying. Listening with half an ear, Amanda watched as Drake walked away. No wonder he wore dark clothes, she thought irrelevantly. The contrast made his hair look like pure honey. Or gold. Fool's gold, she reminded herself, and tore her eyes away.

Across the room Drake and Lina soon fell deep into conversation. She willed him to look over at her, to meet her eyes so that she could see what he was thinking. Who was Drake Daniels, anyway? Was he the sensitive man who had let Lina down so gently and who had seen the difficulties she and her aunt faced at Mount Larkin and arranged to ease them? Or was he the bitter man who had spent thousands of dollars for an opportunity to humiliate her?

But as though determined to keep his secret, he wouldn't look her way. His strong profile was turned to her, so that she could see only his curving lips and his dark fringe of thick lashes as he smiled at Lina. She downed the last of the champagne and felt her head swim, though whether from the drink or from her own hopeless confusion, she wasn't sure.

She knew only that when his hand had touched hers tonight, it had been like the scorch of a brand that marked her forever as his. Whoever he was, saint or sinner, she still loved him and wanted him with a depth of passion that frightened her, one stronger than that which had made her fling aside fear and give herself to him six years ago.

She shuddered at the realization and closed her eyes, trying to find a way out of the impossible dilemma. But her mind still reeled helplessly. She was trapped in the quicksand of the past, and all the struggling she did seemed only to bury her deeper. Even knowing she loved him, she knew she had to make him leave tomorrow. He couldn't stay. Julie was due home next week.

"Okay, everybody, let's light the tree!" Cicely turned the stereo louder, and the benediction of

Christmas bells filled the room as Webster leaned over to plug in the electrical cord.

A murmur of admiration ran through the room as a hundred tiny white lights twinkled to life. Finally, reluctantly, as though against his will, Drake's gaze met hers, and the blaze in his eyes was as bright as the tree beside him. Amanda gripped the back of the nearest armchair as a wave of longing crashed over her.

"Excuse me," she murmured as she moved toward the door. She took Cicely's hand. "I think I'd better turn in now," she said numbly. "I'm tired. It's been a long day."

Cicely's smile was distracted, her attention focused on Webster, who was whispering something into her ear, and Amanda made her exit easily.

She could barely feel the hard stairs beneath her feet as she ascended—her feet were as numb as her mind. Never again, she swore, would she drink like this. Getting pleasantly tipsy was fine for people with nothing to fear. People like Lina just sparkled a little brighter, laughed a little louder. Even her aunt could share one drink too many with Webster and suffer nothing worse than a morning-after headache. But not people like her, people who were hiding from the past, from the future—and from themselves. For her, drinking interfered with her normal control too much, letting in demons of loneliness and misery that she normally kept locked out.

She slid her shaking hand along the wooden banister to brace herself as she struggled up the stairs. A burst of laughter carried from the room behind her, but it sounded weak and distant. She had the feeling she was climbing not a single story but a towering mountain. She felt profoundly alone, the isolation as complete as if she had indeed scaled snowy crystalline heights.

And then she wasn't alone at all. Just as she reached the landing, Drake was behind her, putting his hand on hers.

"Amanda," he said, "we need to talk."

She kept walking blindly. Not now, when her defenses were down. "We can talk tomorrow, Drake." She had reached her own door, and she turned, trying to summon up her earlier bitter pride. "Why don't you just go pack now so you'll be ready to leave first thing in the morning?"

He gripped the ancient molding of the doorway so hard she heard it crack. "You still want me to go?"

"Of course." She raised her brows innocently and brushed a sprinkling of dust from her black bodice.

"And downstairs just now, what was that?"

"Downstairs?" she asked blankly. "I don't know what you mean."

"Like hell you don't!"

She put her hand on the doorknob behind her. "No, I'm sorry, I don't," she repeated with a conciliatory smile, "and if you don't mind, right now I'm very tired. I'd like to go to bed."

He put his hand over hers, so that she couldn't pull the door open. He stood so close that her taffeta skirt rustled against the stiff denim of his jeans. "Please go," she said icily, but she reached out to steady herself on the molding.

Still he didn't move, and her heart raced desperately. She simply couldn't stand this close to him. Already her knees were weak, and she felt a surge of panic within her breast.

"Excuse me, Drake," she said, and reached over to push his arm out of her way. The muscles she encountered were rock hard, immovable.

"Drake?" She looked up into his face and caught her breath. His nostrils were flared with fury, and his eyes were almost black.

"No!" He grabbed her by the upper arms and twisted her up against the wall. His eyes bore into hers even as his fingers ground into her shoulders, and she could smell the bittersweet whiskey on his warm breath.

"I'll show you what I mean." Still holding her against the wall with one hand, he used his other to grab her trembling hand and press it flat against her breast. Her heart stumbled heavily against her palm, and she knew he could feel it, too.

"That's what I mean," he growled under his breath. "I mean you want me. Badly."

Pain shot through her shoulder where he clutched it, but she kept her eyes on his as boldly as she could. Her breath came fast and angry. How dare he use these commando tactics? Though she knew it was foolish, she would not admit anything. It was a battle of wills, and both of them were driven by twin needs— anger's need to dominate and pride's desperate need to resist that domination.

"Go away, Drake," she said scornfully. "You've had too much to drink."

"So have you," he bit back, not relaxing his hold. She tried not to wince. "What does that have to do with anything?"

"Everything," she retorted. "It might make us both say things we'd regret."

"All I want you to say is what your eyes—" he looked down slowly to where their hands joined "—and your heart are already telling me." The husky note that had crept into his voice made her shiver. "You know it's true."

She narrowed her eyes. "And if it were true," she said bitterly, "what then?" Her eyes raked his body contemptuously. "Then would we go in there—" she tilted her head toward her room "—for old time's sake? That may be the way you live, but it's not right for me. Desire isn't enough for me. There has to be—" her voice shook but she steadied it and finished acidly "—something more."

His grip tightened painfully. "More? You mean love? What you felt for your wonderful Richard?"

She shifted helplessly, but his long thighs kept her pinned to the wall. "Love helps," she said tonelessly.

He cursed, low and harsh. "And you don't need this at all, Mandy? You can just walk away from this?" His hands ran roughly across her collarbone to encircle her neck. This time he applied no pressure, but her ragged breathing forced her throat up and down against his hands, and with every deep inhalation she could feel each of his fingers separately, could feel the long hard bones beneath the flesh.

Like a condemned but undaunted prisoner, she stood erect against the wall, unflinching, her eyes bravely locked with his. She thought the combined heat of their flesh would burn her neck. But then he moved his hands again.

His eyes still held her captive, not blinking, while his hot palms slid slowly down her torso. They traced the curving outline of her breasts, and then down and out to her hips. Then up again. And then back down, still slowly.

Though his touch was light, her body's response was immediate and fiery, and she gasped at the eruption of desire that poured hot lava through her. He felt it, too. He continued his rhythmic sweep of her body, increasing the pressure subtly with each stroke, so that his hands were creating need even as they satisfied it, and the touch was never hard enough, never long enough to ease it.

Yes. Yes, she wanted him. Already her body was throbbing with a dull ache, wanting things only he could give her. Her lips tingled, needing the rough pressure of his to cover and control them. But he didn't kiss her. He simply continued his tormenting strokes. The message was clear. To get more she would have to give in, would have to say the words he wanted to hear.

Pride stumbled under desire's raging torrent. Why not say them? He was right. She had already forgotten why she didn't want to admit to needing him. His fingers found her nipples, and she whimpered, finally vanquished.

He pulled away then and stood back, watching her as she folded her hands over her aching breasts.

"If you don't need this, Mandy, then go on in there to bed with your precious memories. But if you do, if you want a real man, real arms, then you know where I am."

A low sob caught in her throat, and she put out her hand toward his broad chest. With lightning reflexes, he caught her wrist in midmotion and held it in a wrenching angry grip.

He held her wrist out from his body, paralyzed in the space between them. "I'm tired of this emotional seesaw. I know you want me. I can feel the need racing in your pulse right now. You want me as much as I want you. But you don't want to admit it to yourself. You want to pretend it isn't happening. You don't have to answer to your grandmother this time, but you still have to answer to yourself, and you don't want to do that, do you? You want to be seduced, so that whatever happens won't be your fault. Maybe you even want to pretend I'm your beloved Richard."

"No." She struggled, her heart pounding. "That's not true."

"Maybe not." He shrugged. "But whatever your motivation, it's not going to be that easy this time. If you make love to me, you're going to know you're doing it. And you're damn well going to know it's me."

He dropped her hand, and as she rubbed it, trying to restore the circulation, he shoved the bedroom door open for her.

"I want you, Amanda," he said, his eyes glittering in the moonlight. "I'm half-mad with it. But I'm leaving. I won't come back here with kisses to drug your conscience into silence. If you want me—and I mean *me*, Mandy, not just a substitute for your dead husband—then you must come to me."

SHE WOULD NOT GO.

Angrily, with a constriction in her throat that was

so painful she could barely swallow, she dragged her zipper down and wrenched the dress over her head. She yanked the green ribbon from her hair and shook the braid until the auburn strands fell free down her back again.

She scrubbed the makeup from her face until it burned. Stripped of the mask of sophistication, it was the face of a child, pink and white and vulnerable. Eyes wide-set, lips full and slightly parted. She would not go.

She pulled an old white nightdress from her top drawer. It was schoolgirlish, just cotton and white eyelet, buttoning up the front, all the way from the floor to her chin. No frothy lace, no shimmering satin, no thigh-high slits, no plunging neckline. She didn't own such things, and she didn't need them anyway. She wasn't dressing for a seduction. She would not go.

Dropping down on the bench in front of the mirror, she dragged the brush through her tangled hair over and over, until it lay like silk on her shoulders. She could read the china clock in the mirror: eleven. It must have been an hour since he left, yet still the muscles in the pit of her stomach were knotted with desire. She drew another deep breath and pressed the stiff bristles of her brush into the palm of her hand.

What was he thinking, as he waited in his room? Did he pace the floor to relax muscles clenched with painful need? Did he begin now to despair, as the minutes ticked by, and rake his fingers through his golden hair? Or had his desire soured into anger now that he knew she wasn't coming?

Still she sat, staring over the top of her dressing table at the wide window. The clouds that had obscured the moon earlier had blown away, and now the full moon hung like a spotlight in the western sky, flooding the trees with a cold silver light. A few snowflakes drifted aimlessly, disappearing before they reached the ground. She watched bleakly, willing the cold to enter her own burning body. She pressed her fists against her belly. Oh, god, when would the fire go out?

As though in answer to her call, the snowflakes began falling harder and faster as the hands of the china clock swept backward in the mirror. In a near trance, she watched without moving, and an hour later, when the two hands met at midnight, the ground was white with snow. The full moon seemed to gaze impassively on a scene as bright as high noon.

But it was a chilling light, and she shivered. Why had she thought the cold was peaceful? She hated winter, which came in glittering silence and buried everything. The last of the emerald-green rye grass, the fallen starbursts of lime-green pine needles, the brave naked branches of chestnut brown, even the crimson of Drake's expensive car—all had been smothered beneath winter's thick shroud.

It would bury her, too, if she let it, and her heart beat faster at the thought of slow suffocation. If she let this winter frost seep into her heart—if she let Drake go with the dawn—then some part of her would be smothered forever. She shivered again as a gust of wind blew the glittering snowflakes at her windowpane, as though seeking admittance. No! She yanked the curtains shut with a frantic tearing gesture.

No! It was summer her soul craved tonight, the high
noon of summer, when the sun sucked perfume from
every flower and flung it improvidently into the air.
Summer, with the ground warm under her back, and
Drake's body hot above her.

She stood up in sudden determination. She might be
mad, but she *would* go to him. Already her breast was
sparking fire again in anticipation. She met her own
eyes in the mirror, and their olive depths held a vital
green. Was this what they used to look like, back when
Drake had gazed deep into them under the summer
sun?

Yes, she would go to him, and together they would
build a fire that would keep out the cold. And if that
fire ended up scorching her heart again, she would
survive.

Without even thinking to check the corridor first,
she flew from the room, her cotton gown billowing
behind her and her auburn hair streaming down her
back. One dim wall fixture glowed in the hall—a
honey light against the creamy wallpaper—and lit the
way to his door.

She didn't knock. She twisted the knob and pushed
the door open.

His room was as bright as daylight, and she took it
all in clearly—the chair drawn up to the window,
where he must have been sitting, watching the snow-
fall, just as she had done, a half-filled suitcase on the
desk, still open. She saw Drake last. He was standing
just inside the closet doorway, a flannel shirt in his
hand. He was wearing only jeans, and his leather belt
was already unbuckled, hanging loose. His feet were

bare, and his naked chest gleamed, all rippled muscle and shadowy hollows in the moonlight.

He didn't speak. He stood rigid, one hand on the door of the closet, and faced her silently.

She eased the door shut behind her.

"I'm cold," she said simply. "I need you to hold me."

The closet door swayed under the force of his convulsive grip, but his face was locked in the same rigid control. "Are you sure?" he asked tonelessly. "I want you to be sure."

For answer, she opened her arms.

Another fraction of a moment he hesitated, and then, flinging his shirt to the floor, he crossed the space between them and gathered her into his arms.

"I had almost given up," he said, bending his head as a tremor passed through him.

She smoothed her trembling fingers over the corded muscles in his chest. "How could I stay away?" she asked, and reaching up, pulled his head down to hers. "Please, Drake. Kiss me."

When their lips met, it was a kiss of more blissful sweetness than any other in her life. His hard mouth moved over hers with such humble tenderness, parted her lips with such gentle solemnity, that tears pooled behind her closed eyes. It was the kind of kiss that dreams are made of, the kind that awakens fairy-tale princesses, the kind that consecrates where it touches.

She thought she could go on forever, just feeling his lips sweeping, warm and healing, over hers, and never need more. But soon, as the sweetness trickled down like honey through her veins, it began to feed a deeper desire. She shifted her body against his in an instinctive rhythm and felt the rigid contours of his masculinity.

In answer his fingers moved to the top of her gown. His knuckles grazed the sensitive underside of her chin as they loosened the first pearly button. And then the second, and the third, until the throbbing pulse at the base of her throat had been exposed.

With fluid grace he sank to his knees and slowly released the rest of the pearly beads, one by one, until her gown hung open. She wore nothing underneath, and he knelt before her, his eyes worshiping every inch of creamy skin lit between the shadows.

The throbbing knot she had felt in the pit of her stomach now was aching unendurably. He drew his hands slowly up her legs, from her calves to the sensitive curves behind her knees, and up her thighs to rest possessively on her narrow waist. She marveled at his patient deliberation. Her need for him was screaming through every vein, and reaching down, she wound her fingers into his fair hair.

"Love me," she whispered. "Love me, Drake."

His hands slipped down to cup the firm softness of her buttocks, and he moved his face forward until it was lost in the shadows of her open gown. She gasped, as though a searing flame had licked at her heart, as she felt first his breath, warm and quick upon her stomach, and then his lips, pressing light kisses on the soft quivering flesh.

The gentle touch seemed to twist cruelly at the muscles of her abdomen, and breathless, she bent over his head, digging her hands more tightly into his golden hair. Her body seemed to beat a hot, slow, primitive drumming as his lips slid down her stomach.

And then, as if the creeping fire had suddenly reached a forgotten storehouse of explosives, her entire body combusted. Her head fell back, and she uttered a small cry as fire shot through her, through her torso and into her arms and legs, consuming as it went. Muscles melted in the flame, and only his hard fingers against her hips kept her from falling.

Even when the fire receded, she wasn't sure she could stand alone. Her shaking fingers still clasped his hair, as she steadied herself on the strong head that rested now against her belly. Her legs trembled against his naked chest, and sensing the movement, he rose quickly to his feet and scooped her into his arms. Her gown fell wide open, revealing her swollen breasts to the moonlight, but she felt no shame. She let her head rest upon his chest as he carried her to the bed, and she felt the wild tripping of his heart against her ear.

He placed her gently on top of the satin quilt and stood up. For an instant she panicked, afraid he was leaving. Did he think the fire had died? Did he not realize another fire was already building inside her, that she needed him more than ever?

"Drake," she said, holding out her hand, "come back."

But he was only sliding his jeans down along his legs, along the thick ribbons of corded muscles that she remembered so well. She watched, her heart knocking at her throat as the moonlight revealed the beloved body that for six long years she had seen only in dreams. It was just as she remembered it, the broad shoulders and lean hips, the golden curves and dusky shadows, the grace of its utterly masculine power. A ripple of urgent need shook through her.

Finally he stood naked before her, and she knew that he would not—could not—leave her now.

And still he was gentle and slow, though his deliberate movements now had a sense of urgency about them, as though he were struggling to contain some wild inner force. He moved onto the bed beside her and, slipping between her legs, carefully laid aside the folds of her gown.

"You are so beautiful." Reverently he laid his palms against her breasts. The nipples puckered under the enfolding heat, and he kneaded them softly.

"Did you know I have made love to you every day in my books?" he asked. Her eyes widened, and he nodded. "Yes, I have. Every day, with words, I have worshiped your eyes, your hair, your fire...." He dipped his mouth to her breast and ran his hard tongue around the stiff peak. "That's why my heroine has no name, none that I can tell the world. Her name is Amanda."

She moaned and shifted under his hot touch. The fire was crackling inside her again. "I never forgot a thing about you, Mandy," he said, his lips hot against her breast. "I wouldn't let myself. But finally, words were not enough. I had to see you again." He pressed against her, and she felt each muscled inch of him straining toward her. "I had to hold you again.

"Oh, Mandy, it's been so long," he groaned and, wrapping his arms hard behind her back, crushed her to him.

Then there was no more room for words as he drank from the fire of her lips and became a part of the fire that raged within her. This was not the eager innocent exploration of their earlier coupling. Six years of hopeless thirst had parched their passion, and need swept through them like a brushfire. Out of control, the flames soared to lick the sky.

And then there was another explosion, this one violent enough to rock the stars.

When it had passed, leaving only quivering tremors behind, they lay without moving, exhausted. Her head fit perfectly into the curve of his arm, and his hand lay protectively across her shoulder. She was utterly tranquil, sated, but even so her body felt a lingering glow where he had possessed her. She didn't move a muscle, afraid to break the spell, and his breathing eased slowly, until she thought he was asleep.

But suddenly he spoke.

"And you, Amanda—did you ever think of me?" he asked quietly. "In all those years, did you ever wish I were here, lying beside you?"

She didn't look at him, for in that instant tears had welled up in her eyes. She nodded slowly, hoping not to spill them onto his chest.

"Yes," she whispered. The glow was still strong as her mind began functioning again. Gently he lifted her face to his. She could see him clearly in the abnormally white midnight. His blue eyes still burned, and his hands caressed her neck.

"Just yes?" he said thickly, a small smile on his swollen lips. "Just a simple yes?"

She lifted her hands to his brow and smoothed away the perspiration that matted his fair hair. "Yes, I wanted you. I want you still." She dropped her hands to his chest, where she stroked his hardening nipples. "That's simple, isn't it?"

He breathed deeply, and her hands rose and fell in the moonlight with his motions, and she felt they were nearly made of the same body. She felt his heart speed up under her restless fingertips.

"No," he said, and with a low groan he swept her into his arms again and crushed her against his pounding heart. "No, it's far from simple, but just for tonight let us pretend it is."

Just for tonight. Dimly she heard the words. But right now her body was listening only to the wild wind that tore through her, sweeping all other sounds from its path. And as his body joined hers again, the words spun helplessly away, caught in passion's black storm.

CHAPTER EIGHT

HOURS LATER, when she woke, he was gone, though the bed was still warm under her fingers where his body had lain. She stretched as her fingers probed, and peeked sleepily through her lashes at the empty room. She had no clear sense of the passage of time, but the light that filled the room was rosy now. It was night no longer.

Where was he? Downstairs, perhaps, getting something to eat?

Her tired body relaxed back into the warm sheets. She could still see through her lashes the half-packed suitcase that lay on the desk beside the door, but the sight had lost its power to terrorize her. He would not be leaving now. How could he? They had spent the night in each other's arms, making love over and over, until it seemed they were the single, focused center of a world that spun wildly around them. Though he had, toward morning, finally slept, she had lain awake beside him for a while longer, watching the deep rise and fall of his chest, memorizing the way his rugged profile looked in the moonlight.

No, though they had never talked about what the future would hold, she couldn't believe that he could just walk away from what they had found last night.

But what, a tiny voice inside her asked, exactly was it they had found? All too clearly she remembered the words he had used last night to describe his characters, and her fingers curled into her palms in a spasm of sudden anxiety. "They don't have love," he had said. "They have only need and a kind of driven desire."

She took a deep ragged breath. If she had been the model for his heroine, then— Hadn't desire consumed them both tonight? But never a word had been spoken about love.

Well, she had known that when she came to him. He had never promised her love. Just real arms. Real need. A real man. She turned her face into the damp hollow of the pillow and drank deeply of the beautiful musty odor of him.

Determinedly she relaxed her hands, smoothing them over the linen pillowcase. No, it was more than that. He couldn't have held her the way he had unless he loved her. His touch had been reverent, not merely lustful. Every kiss had been sweet with promise, even though no words had been spoken. His possession had been complete, encompassing her soul as well as her body.

They had both felt it, she was sure of it. And now, she knew, it was time to give their feelings words. She gripped the pillow hard, its softness bending under her tense fingers. It wouldn't be easy. There were so many things she had to tell him, things about her marriage, about her life in the years without him.

Yesterday she would have said it was impossible. The gulf had seemed too wide, too treacherous, ever to cross. But today, with the memory of his touch still burning in her, she was sure they could find a way. Somehow, together, they could build a bridge between the past and the future, a bridge that would carry them safely over the pain and loneliness of the six long years that had separated them.

Suddenly impatient, she sat up and pulled on her gown, covering her bare breasts. A sense of urgency overwhelmed her. She hurried to her own room, glad that no one else had awakened yet. She and Drake needed time alone to talk. She let her nightgown drop in a soft white heap around her feet and threw on the first clothes that her urgent fingers encountered—a gray woolen dress she had left out to take to the cleaners. It didn't matter what she wore. It mattered only that she get to him quickly, that she feel again his hard hands against her back, pulling her toward him, see again the tenderness in his blue eyes. She needed to know she had not imagined it.

She didn't even stop to brush her hair—she just raked her fingers carelessly through it as she descended the stairs. Already her arms ached for him, as if it had been years rather than hours since they had made love. But they had so much time to make up for, she told herself as her feet flew across the stairs. They might never drink their fill of each other.

The nutty smell of brewing coffee reached her halfway down, and she knew she had been right. He was making breakfast.

"Morning," she called tentatively as she reached the kitchen door. But when she stepped across the threshold, she saw that the big kitchen was empty except for the gurgle of the brewing coffee and a white wicker tray set with two coffee cups and napkins.

Her heart lurched at the homey sight. Wouldn't it be wonderful to share such simple domestic pleasures with him for the rest of her life? If only they could get through the next few hours, if only she could make him understand everything that had happened, then finally they could find their future together.

"Drake?" She peered into the pantry, which was dark and silent. The emptiness threw her slightly off balance. Where had he gone?

She opened the kitchen door briefly, just long enough to see that his car, which wore the snow like a mink jacket, still waited in the driveway. Shivering against the quick whip of wind, she closed the door and called his name again.

And then she saw him. He was in the living room, bending down beside the bookcase, just as she had been when he found her last night. Her eager greeting died on her lips as she saw her black portfolio lying empty on the coffee table. Her breath froze in her throat as she saw the blue-gold sketches splayed across the carpet at his feet.

Her sketches! Her heart did a slow swoop down through her body, even though from this distance she couldn't be sure which pictures they were. The golden hair and cobalt-blue eyes could have belonged to either the handsome man or the beautiful little girl.

Dread coursed through her veins like poison. *No, Drake, no!* she cried inwardly. *Not yet. Not before I explain.* She tore her eyes away from the scattered pictures to look more closely at him. He was squatting, his elbows on his knees and his hands in his tangled hair, and staring down at the sketches blankly.

Something in his lost, bewildered posture told her exactly which pictures they were. They were of Julie.

So it was already too late—too late for those gentle explanations she had anticipated so eagerly just moments ago. Too late to offer the news with pride and shaky joy, like a gift. Amanda's heart twisted and her legs went numb. He already knew. Probably he had known instantly.

It would be Julie's eyes, of course, that had told him—those unusual cobalt-blue eyes that enchanted everyone who saw her. Lots of little girls had that softly golden hair, but only Drake's daughter could have those strange and wonderful eyes.

Amanda had sometimes fancied that Drake had left the best of himself behind in those eyes—that which was warm and loyal and good in him had lingered at Mount Larkin to bloom again in Julie's eyes, while the greedy treacherous side of him had disappeared forever into an autumn night.

It had even seemed sometimes that in that small way she had managed to cheat fate. Now, as she saw the rigid tension in Drake's broad back, she saw that it was just another of fate's wicked tricks. Because she had never expected to see Drake again, she had never realized until this very moment what danger lay in Julie's beautiful eyes. As she watched him now, hunched over her pictures of his daughter, fear passed through her like a wind of nausea, leaving her weak and trembling. For a moment she didn't speak at all, and then she whispered his name.

"Drake..." she said, like a prayer.

Startled at the sound, he looked up, and his eyes were blank, baffled, like those of a sleeper just awakened. He stared at her a long moment.

"She's mine, isn't she?" When he finally spoke, his voice was muffled, as though it came from across a great distance. "She's my daughter."

She hesitated only briefly and then she nodded.

He stared down at the sketches again, letting his fingers sift slowly from one to the other, comparing and confirming. She watched helplessly, trying to find words.

Suddenly he cursed and whipped his head around like a snapped lariat. His eyes were filled with dazzling fury.

"How could you?" His voice was violent. "For the love of god, how could you?" He held up one of the sketches, and she stepped back, as if he'd brandished a gleaming sabre.

Her breath caught in her lungs and she couldn't answer. With the ominous grace of a predator, he sprang to his feet, dropping the picture, and stalked toward her.

"All right, Amanda," he said, between clenched teeth, his voice edged so sharp it cut the air between them, "this time I want the truth. When is her birthday?"

Amanda swallowed hard, but her voice had disappeared and she couldn't speak.

He narrowed his eyes to cold blue slits. "Dammit—answer me!" He flung the words at her, and when she didn't speak he reached out and grabbed her upper arms in his punishing hands. "*When* was she born?"

"In the spring," Amanda whispered painfully, forcing the words through her frozen throat. "In April. April tenth. Right in the middle of azalea time." She almost laughed, but she choked on the tears instead. "She loves the azaleas. She thinks they bloom for her birthday." She looked away, unable to bear the hatred in his eyes. "You never saw the azaleas, did you, Drake? You had been gone seven months when Julie was born. Seven months and three days."

His fingers seemed to pierce her skin as he stared at her. His eyes were like lethal black whirlpools, and she shut her own to avoid drowning in them.

"April tenth? Then you already knew, didn't you? The last time we were together, before I left...you knew."

Again she nodded. She hadn't known for sure, but what else could she say? The time for deception had run out. The hourglass was smashed.

"My god!"

She winced as his grip tightened. She could almost hear the grinding of his fingers against her fragile bones.

"All these years..." The words spilled out of him. "It's funny, really. I tried to understand. I knew you were young and spoiled and greedy for life. I told myself it made sense. You just weren't able to give up being the wealthy Miss Larkin, and you'd rather do without me than go without the luxuries you were accustomed to."

He cursed again. "I hated it. I hated *you*. But when I came here, I was fool enough to think maybe you had changed. And last night I was even ready to forgive you for everything, to forgive you for the six years of emptiness I endured.''

She sobbed, tears rolling fat and hot down her cheeks. Did he not realize how empty and hopeless her life had been, too? Or was that really true? At least she'd had Julie.

"But Drake, I—" she began, strangling on the words.

"I'm not finished!" His words ripped into her struggling explanation. "But you weren't even going to tell me now, were you? Not even after last night. Last night didn't mean a damn thing to you, did it? And I thought..."

He didn't finish the sentence, just shook her violently, his voice rising to a boiling fury. "Don't you see what you did? You stole my daughter—for a few miserable party dresses, a couple of trips to Europe. You stole my daughter."

For a moment his eyes glittered so brightly she thought he might cry, too, and she almost forgave him his fury. Suppose *she* had spent the last six years without Julie? Suppose somehow she now had to face the fact that her daughter didn't even know her? Her tears came faster, hotter, and she began to cry out loud. "Oh, Drake, I'm sorry. I'm so sorry—"

He let go of her arms with a vengeance and flung her away from him.

"Do you think *that* is going to change anything now? Are you still such a child that you think you can say 'I'm sorry' and I'll forgive you for anything—even this?"

"You don't understand," she said.

"You're damn right I don't," he spat. "Where I come from there may not have been much money, but there was enough human decency that no one would do this to a dog."

"I thought you didn't care!" she cried. "You went away... just drove away. I couldn't stop you."

"Oh, sure, and I'll bet you tried real hard, didn't you? Whenever you had the time, what with the wedding plans and all."

"I did try," she murmured, unconsciously fingering the scar behind her knee. "I did try."

"Liar!" He pounded the wall with his fist. "It was only a few weeks later that I got the letter from Olivia—the announcement of your wedding. 'Just in case I had any illusions left,' she said. Damn you, Mandy." His voice broke. "Damn you for not even having the courage to tell me yourself."

"How could I?" she cried, stung finally into speech. "What was I supposed to say if I called you? I couldn't beat my grandmother's offer."

He stopped short, his volcanic fury cooling into an icy rock, which was no less dangerous for being cold.

"Because you thought you didn't have to. You thought your grandmother had gotten rid of me for you." He raked his eyes up and down her body with unveiled disgust. His gaze stopped, narrowing, fixing on a spot near her waist.

"Is that the money, Amanda?" With an angry thrust, he reached into the pocket of her dress and pulled out a piece of paper. Her eyes widened. It was the check she had written at the restaurant. "You see? You could better her offer, couldn't you? You managed to double it today."

Her cheeks flamed as she realized what he must be thinking. It had never occurred to her in her eager haste that she was putting on the same dress she'd worn that fateful day, but he clearly believed she'd come down to pay him off. Oh, god, why had she left the damned thing in her pocket? How could he think that she had really meant to offer it to him? After last night could he possibly believe she still wanted him to leave?

"I didn't..." Her heart frozen, she didn't know where to begin defending herself. "I wasn't trying to steal her, Drake—"

He interrupted with a short bark of grim laughter. "What then? Buy her?" He crumpled the check in a huge, white-knuckled fist. "Don't you dare even utter the words! My god, you Larkins are monstrous. Do you think that having money entitles you to do whatever you want with other people's lives? Did you really think that because you were old Olivia Larkin's heiress you had the right to steal my daughter? There's just one little thing you and your grandmother didn't realize. You can't buy people. She's my daughter, and she always will be."

He came back to her, his face rigid with a hard-won control. "I want you to call her. Right now." His words came like the crack of a whip. "Tell that man to bring her home. Today."

"I won't," she gasped brokenly. "You'll frighten her. I won't let you upset her."

He narrowed his eyes, and his rugged face looked all angles, all cruelty. "You can't order me around anymore, Miss Amanda. Don't forget, it's my house, too." He laughed at her sharp gasp, and it was as mirthless as laughter risen straight from hell. "Yes, it's a wonderful, twisted justice, isn't it? You know those azaleas our daughter loves so much? Well, they're mine now."

Still laughing harshly, he strode to the counter and picked up the coffee cup he had set out for her earlier. He looked at it as though it contained poison and with a muttered curse flung it against the cabinet. It broke into a hundred pieces.

"Yes. I'll give her one for her birthday—now that I know when it is. You just make sure you get her here."

And with that he shoved the door open and left the house.

MARTIN, full of curiosity but cooperative, agreed to bring Julie home, though he said they couldn't get a plane until later that evening. Hanging up reluctantly, Amanda stopped by Drake's door to let him know, but he hadn't returned. Relieved, she left a terse message on his desk, including only the time the travelers were expected and a note reminding him that Julie would be very tired and should go straight to bed.

The rest of the day passed in a blur. She was like a computer programmed to perform routine chores. Cauterized by the burning emotions, she felt almost nothing. After clearing up the broken cup, she began breakfast, which was followed by the dreaded conferences with Cicely and Webster, who had to be told the whole miserable story. And then, while Webster comforted a horrified Cicely, Amanda stumbled through the usual work of running the house.

She worked frenetically all day. Though exhausted from emotional strain and lack of sleep she was glad

to be busy—too busy to think. Thinking was too
painful. Whenever, at a quiet moment, Drake or Julie flashed into her consciousness, it was like knives
slashing at the carefully patched fabric of her life.
Time and again she pushed the pain away and tackled
another chore.

After several hours Drake returned. From the window in one of the upstairs bedrooms, as she shook a
pillow into its fresh case, she saw the Jaguar's hood
thrust aggressively toward the house. Even before
Drake turned off the engine, Webster appeared in the
yard, and she watched with the peculiar emotional
distance of one who was merely a spectator at a play
as the two men talked. Webster's face was lined with
worry; Drake's was as hard as a smooth golden stone.
Finally Drake moved away, approaching the house,
leaving Webster frowning thoughtfully after him.

Even through her emotional paralysis, she felt a
rush of warmth for Webster. Thank goodness he was
here today, when Cicely needed his strength and comfort more than ever. She herself could have been no
help at all to her aunt.

Later Amanda fixed dinner, but excused herself
from eating it, instead delivering a tray to her aunt's
room and then going into Julie's room to prepare it for
her little girl's arrival.

Tears pricked at her eyes as she straightened the
fluffy white quilt and sat the brown bear up a little
straighter. What would Julie, who in her short life had
known nothing but love, think of all of this? She had
always accepted Amanda's story that, though her real
father couldn't live with them, he still loved her dearly.

She had hoped Julie would be much older before she had to explain in detail about Drake. But now...

Amanda dropped onto the edge of the bed, in the ivory pool of light from the small bedside lamp, absently stroking the soft brown bear. Maybe it would be all right. Julie was such an accepting child. Her unusual life of meeting new people every week, as Mount Larkin's visitors came and went, had made her so. She probably would accept Drake, too, if only he would be gentle.

But would he be? Though he had changed a great deal in the past six years, Drake *could* be gentle—last night had proved that. She could almost feel the touch of his hands, gliding up her neck, behind her ear and into her hair. Perhaps, even though he felt such rage toward her, he would call on that softer, kinder side when he met his daughter tonight.

"It's almost nine o'clock."

She looked up blankly. She had neglected to turn on the hall light, and Drake was standing in the shadows at the doorway. She couldn't see his face, and his voice was too low and controlled to give anything away.

"Is it—already?" Her fingers dug into the bear's fur. Julie's plane had landed at eight, and Martin had insisted that Amanda not try to maneuver through the snow to meet them. "I'll get her home safely," he had promised. "You just keep the light burning."

Well, the lights were burning, and Julie would be arriving any minute. Suddenly Amanda felt hopelessly unprepared. She had no formula ready to meet this moment. She had been so certain Drake was out of her life forever. She hadn't, until he appeared at her door only a week ago, ever dreamed this day would come.

"I need to know what you've told her." Drake moved a foot or two into the room and stopped, sending his gaze over the small white bookcase, the yellow toy chest, the bed on which Amanda sat. "About who her father is."

"Not much," she answered dully. "She's still so little, and it was so complicated...." She picked up the bear and hugged him to her chest like a shield against the pain. "I've always said that her daddy—" her voice shook on the word "—wasn't able to live with us. But that you loved her very much."

He fingered the picture books that lined the little case. "You never told her, then, that your husband was her father?"

Amanda shook her head dumbly. Richard had wanted her to, had been so sure it would be the simplest way, but somehow she hadn't been able to do it.

Drake turned his brooding eyes on her, and his voice was strangely impersonal. "Thank you for that, at least."

She stood up then, tossing the little bear back onto the pillow. "I didn't do it for you," she said tautly, and went to stand at the window.

He didn't answer, and they stood that way several minutes, the air between them humming with tension. Finally, just when Amanda felt she could stand it no longer, the yellow light of a taxi swept into the drive. She watched it maneuver the curving turns, like a small golden star that rolled unerringly to her door. And then she turned.

"She's here," she said, her voice tight. "And Drake... you have to be patient. I can't tell her tonight. You'll have to give me time."

"Take all the time you want," he said darkly. "After six years I can wait a few more days."

Then he stood back, his hand extended to allow her to pass through the doorway first.

CHAPTER NINE

"MOMMY!"

The long-feared moment, when it finally came, had the simplicity of the inevitable. Julie dropped her Mickey Mouse toy, which was almost as big as she was, on the foyer floor and ran straight for her mother. Her smiling face was sun-browned from her weeks in Florida, and her eyes looked startlingly blue against the tan.

Drake and Martin watched silently as Amanda fell to her knees to embrace her little girl. She had meant to introduce Drake right away, but it had been so long and so much had happened since she had last held her daughter. She buried her face in Julie's soft fine hair.

"Hi, sweetheart," she said, choking back tears. "I missed you so much."

"Me, too." Julie's embrace was happy, but casual. She obviously didn't sense any of the emotional undertones that held the grown-ups in such a paralyzing lock. She didn't know she was the chief pawn in their mysterious game. She thought she was just a little girl. Pulling away, she looked toward the stairs.

"Where's Auntie Cicely?" As she looked around, for the first time she caught sight of Drake, and she hesitated, looking momentarily disconcerted. Her hand crept back into Amanda's.

"Julie, Martin—this is Drake," Amanda said, struggling to her feet. "He's one of our guests."

Amanda could feel Drake's tension at the inadequate explanation, but Julie's smile brightened. That put Drake into a perspective she could understand. There were always guests at Mount Larkin.

"Hi," she said and looked back down the hall. "Where's Cicely?" she asked again. "Is she upstairs? Can I go show her what I got you for Christmas?"

"Sure, honey." Amanda stroked her hair. "She's been waiting for you. Give her a big kiss."

As Julie flew up the wide sweep of stairs, calling her aunt, Amanda turned to Martin. "Thanks," she said, enfolding him in a hug, "for bringing her so quickly."

Martin just nodded, tossing Drake a quick look out of the corners of his brown eyes. He obviously had understood the implications of those two pairs of deep blue eyes. "To tell you the truth, she was getting a little homesick." He looked searchingly at her. "You okay?"

"Yes," she assured him. "Fine."

She still held Martin's hand, but her attention was fixed on Drake, who was standing, his stiff back to them, staring at the empty stairs. Amanda's heart squeezed, sensing instinctively his frustration and pain. She knew it was better for Julie to take him for granted at first, to accept him casually as a guest before she had to grapple with their more intimate relationship, but she also knew how hard that was for him. To see your own child for the first time and to have her dismiss you with one indifferent syllable . . . It twisted her heart to imagine how much that must hurt.

"Drake," she said and put her hand out to touch the rigid muscles in his shoulders. In the bright light from the chandelier his hair looked as soft as Julie's, and for one crazy moment she had the urge to smooth it soothingly, the way she had done so many times for her daughter.

Then he turned on his heel, and she dropped her hand instantly. In this mood, with the fire of rage burning behind his eyes, he couldn't have looked less like the smiling Julie.

"Am I supposed to thank you now? For my two minutes of fatherhood?"

"N-no," she said falteringly. "Of course not."

"Good." He pushed past her, ignoring both her pleading look and Martin's frown. "Because I'm not feeling very grateful."

He wrenched the door open, and a snow flurry blew past him, making her shiver. He strode out the door, across the porch and down to the path, his boots crunching angrily on the snow. Turning, he stood for a moment like a wrathful pillar of fire rising out of the frozen ground. "Tell her soon, Amanda. I won't wait forever."

THE SNOW CONTINUED to fall like magic dust sprinkled from a fairy's wand, and for the next few days everyone was content to stay indoors, playing Christmas carols on the stereo and wrapping presents behind closed doors.

Much to Amanda's relief, Drake didn't approach her or Julie directly at all. He seemed content, for now at least, to be just one of the crowd, a quietly smiling presence that Julie gradually came to take for granted.

His deep baritone joined the other voices raised in "Silent Night." His finger held down silver ribbons as bows were tied, and he collected baskets of baby pinecones for decorations. His long arms maneuvered the brass poker to revive a dying fire, or cradled thick, sweet-smelling logs to lay a new one. He even stood beside Amanda in the kitchen, creating a cinnamon-scented cider to drink with her homemade vegetable soup.

As Christmas approached, the time came for Lina and Tom to leave, and Drake stood at the door, waving goodbye with the rest of them. No new guests arrived. With the exception of Webster, Cicely and Amanda never accepted guests over Christmas—not the wisest financial decision perhaps, but they both felt that Julie should be surrounded only by family on that important day.

No one mentioned Drake's continued presence. Cicely, of course, avoided confrontation energetically, usually managing to be at the opposite end of the house. Martin, too, kept his distance, apparently not having forgiven Drake for his outburst on that first night. Of them all, only Webster spent any time alone with Drake. The two men talked in desultory, late-night fashion over long, fireside chess games. Amanda had no idea what they said.

She retired early each night, tucking Julie in after reading her a chapter of *The Snow Queen*, and then lying on her own bed, trying not to think of the past or the future or the man who even now was sitting in her living room, chin in hand, studying the chessboard in front of him. She tried not to think of how the amber firelight would play across his face, lighting the hollows between strong jaw and high cheek-bones, or of how his lean fingers would caress the smooth ivory of the queen as he moved her into place.

But one night the chess game ended early, and Drake appeared at Julie's door just as she and Amanda were picking out a new book; they had finished *The Snow Queen* the night before.

Amanda started as his dark shadow fell into the room, but Julie smiled over at him. "Hi, Drake," she said, and Amanda tried to smile, too.

"Hi." His gaze went to the bookcase, where Amanda was sitting, cross-legged, reading the spines of a hundred possibilities. "Looking for a good book?"

She nodded, not meeting his eye. "It's not easy. We've read them all so many times," she rambled nervously, explaining too much. "I think Julie knows them by heart."

"Well, I've got an idea." He sat on the edge of Julie's bed, smiling. Julie sat up straighter, sensing with a child's unerring instinct that bedtime might be postponed a bit tonight.

"What?" she urged shamelessly.

"Why don't we make up one? Your mommy tells me you like to make up stories, and so do I." He smiled over at Amanda, the first personal, unambivalent smile she'd had from him in a long time. Her heart began to race foolishly, and she breathed deeply to control its pace. It's only for Julie's sake, she told herself raggedly. It's like a game of charades, and we're acting out the part of happy parents.

"Okay." Julie looked a little shy but interested.

And then Drake began to spin a tale, a simple and charming story of a Christmas present that got lost and wasn't found until many years later. He would start a sentence and then let Julie finish it. As the story got wilder and sillier and Julie's laughter became less self-conscious, Amanda found herself chuckling, too.

Leaning against the bookcase and watching from her position on the floor, she found herself wishing the moment would never end. The two blond heads bent together, the two pairs of blue eyes sparkling. It was a sight she had thought she would never see.

And then Drake's smiling eyes turned her way. "Let's ask Mommy," he was suggesting, and she realized that, lost in her profound appreciation of the moment, she had not been listening. But it didn't matter—there was something in the easy way he called her Mommy that tugged at her heart. She felt tears well up in her eyes, and the two expectant faces looking at her began to blur.

"I...I don't know," she stammered, unsure of what to do. She didn't want to cry in front of Julie, who would never understand. She stumbled to her feet, clumsy in her haste.

"I think I'd better go," she managed. "I'll come to check on you later, honey."

She dropped a kiss on Julie's forehead and hurried from the room, reaching the hall just in time. She pushed her shaking hands hard against her rapidly filling eyes, so hard she saw a spider's web of light behind her lids.

How could she go on playing at this parody of a family? How long could she live under the same roof with Drake, loving him, wanting him and knowing how he hated her? How could she bear to watch his love for Julie grow every hour, and know that he would never feel the same love for her?

She tilted her head back against the wall and let the tears seep slowly out of the corners of her eyes and trickle away unseen. He clearly intended to be a father, a good father, and she should be glad. Julie needed a father. But oh, god—Amanda's throat constricted in a strangled sob—oh, god, she needed him, too!

"You hate it, don't you?"

Surprised by the curt voice, Amanda straightened up, wiping at the moisture that had trickled to her hairline. She hadn't expected him to come out so soon, but she tried to sound composed. "Hate what?"

Drake took her elbow roughly and moved her away from Julie's closed door. He led her down the long hall, toward Amanda's room.

"You hate to see me with her."

Amanda pulled her elbow away. "No—of course I don't." She hoped the tears hadn't thickened her voice too much. She rested her hand on her doorknob lightly, hinting she wanted to withdraw.

Drake's face darkened. "Oh, yes, you do. I can see it every time I'm with her. You have to turn your eyes away. You worked so hard to keep me from her, and now you just can't stand that she's beginning to know me, to care about me."

Amanda turned her side to him and twisted the knob. "You're imagining things. And now if you'll excuse me—"

"Well, I won't!" He grabbed her hand and stayed it. "I'm warning you, Amanda. You are just going to have to make the best of this. That little girl is my daughter, and I'm going to make her love me if it takes the rest of my life. And if you try to interfere, however subtly..."

The pressure on her hand increased threateningly, and Amanda felt her own anger rising with it.

"I won't get in your way, Drake," she said through clenched teeth. "But I want you to understand one thing. If you do it, if you make her love you, then there's no turning back. It will be too late to decide you'd really rather be the footloose Roger Stowe. Don't try coming to me then and asking for your goodbye check."

He let go of her, as though her cold hand had burned him, and she took advantage of her freedom to whip open the door and step into the sanctuary of her room.

"Don't forget I've had the privilege of seeing you in action before," she bit back. "I know what you're capable of, Drake, and I'm warning you not to try it. A summer lover is one thing—but there's no such thing as a summer father. Either you're her father forever—or you get out now."

With that she slammed the door on his taut face. She leaned against it, her heart pounding like a jackhammer in her chest, and listened. At first there was silence, as though he stood motionless on the other side. And then there were footsteps, slow and heavy, receding down the hall.

She slept fitfully. All night the dream repeated itself relentlessly. Like a nicked record she ran and called and fell, then ran and called and fell again. When she finally awoke, she was damp with perspiration and utterly exhausted. And it was Christmas Eve.

She had to force herself to do her exercises, then dressed indifferently in a fleecy sweat suit of periwinkle blue. A dreary sense of foreboding seemed to hang over her, and she couldn't shake it.

She was in the kitchen when she heard the screaming.

From the first shrill note she knew it was Julie. Dropping the bowl of eggs she had been beating, she raced toward the door and flew out into the snow-covered yard. Julie! Where was she?

Another cry rang out in the cold clear air. It came from the far edge of the property. Ignoring the stab of pain in her right leg, Amanda ran toward the sound. *Please, please,* her thoughts chanted. *Let her be all right.*

She rounded the corner just as another shrill cry died on the air, and then she saw them. Drake was pushing a shiny red sled, and Julie, bedecked in a new rabbit-fur coat and hat, was riding it, shrieking gleefully, her blond hair escaping from the hat and flying in the wind.

With a sense of horror, Amanda saw her daughter sliding down the hill—that wretched hill, the one that had, six years ago, almost destroyed them both.

"No! Stop! *Stop!*" She raced after the gleaming red sled, but she knew she couldn't catch it. It was skimming easily over the clean snow, falling, falling . . . right into Webster's waiting arms.

Breathless, Amanda reached him just seconds after Julie did, and she grabbed the little girl, hugging her with relief even while she scolded.

"Didn't I tell you never to play on this hill? Didn't you know this is off-limits, Julie? You should never, never have done this without asking Mommy." She breathed the new scent of the rabbit-fur hat and squeezed Julie until she squirmed away.

"Drake said it was okay, Mommy. He bought me this new sled, and this new coat, too."

Drake had reached them now, his face tense above the lush white Irish sweater that made his broad shoulders look enormous. "What's the matter, Mandy?"

Even Webster looked worried, and Amanda began to feel foolish. When she and Julie had come to live here, they had put a fence along the bottom of the hill, blocking off the road. And Julie would have been safe anyway, with Webster waiting only halfway down the hill. Julie had never been anywhere near the road.

All the same, it had terrified her. The hill always terrified her. It represented so much loss, so much pain.

"I'm sorry," she said awkwardly. "I didn't realize Webster was there to catch you, honey. Mommy was just worried. Tell you what—why don't you try sledding on the other side of the house? The hill isn't as steep there."

Julie pouted. "I want to ride here." Amanda turned, ready to assert parental authority. Drake was spoiling her.

But in an instant Drake had scooped Julie up into his arms.

"Hey! Mommy said no," he said, holding her so high she giggled with delight. "Try the other side.

You've already got this side all figured out, anyhow. It's time for a new challenge."

He set Julie down and rumpled her hair affectionately. "Okay?"

"Okay." Her sunny nature prevailed, and she took Webster's hand and headed up the hill, dragging the sled behind them.

Drake turned, as though to join them, but halted when Amanda touched his arm. "I want to talk to you," she said curtly. He nodded and watched as the other two made their way slowly through the snow toward the house. When they were clearly out of earshot, he turned back to Amanda.

As he looked at her face, which she knew must be white and shaken, she saw his expression soften. He came closer and put a gentle arm around her. "What's the matter, Mandy?" he repeated softly, wiping the perspiration from her brow with a gloved hand. "Why are you so frightened?"

She hated the way her body melted at his slightest touch, and hoped he couldn't see it. "I'm not frightened," she contradicted flatly, jerking out of his embrace. "I'm angry. Julie knows she's not supposed to play on this hill, and she should have asked me. In the future check with me before you do anything so dangerous. You may buy her toys now, Drake, but I still make the rules. Do you understand that?"

Rebuffed, he stared at her without answering, his lids heavy over stony blue eyes. Anger was visible in every muscle.

"We'll talk about it later," he said finally.

"It's not open for discussion," she said coldly, turning away to look at the hill. "And another thing.

That hat and coat are totally inappropriate for a child Julie's age. They must have cost more than everything else she has put together."

"Good," he said angrily, grabbing her arm and pulling her back to face him. "There's nothing wrong with that. I intend for her to have the best of everything."

With a grunt of frustration he grabbed both her arms and drew her close, but she held herself rigid in his grasp.

"Why are you being so difficult? I love her, Mandy. Don't you see that? I want to make her happy, do things for her, the way all daddies do things for their little girls. Don't shut me out. Let me love her."

Amanda pursed her lips, hardening her heart against the earnest sound in his voice. "Money isn't the same thing as love, Drake," she bit back. "She doesn't need your money. She doesn't need expensive new clothes and toys. She was perfectly happy before you and your money ever showed up."

He narrowed his eyes. "And she'd be happy again if we left? Is that what you're trying to tell me?"

She almost said yes, but honesty prevailed. "No..." she said, haltingly, grudgingly. "No, I think she'd miss you if you left now."

It wasn't exactly an effusive compliment, and he never could have guessed how much it cost her to admit it. Julie *had* grown to care for Drake, so quietly, so naturally, that it was as though blood spoke to blood in some wordless way. Amanda knew she could never come between them now, and she would never want to. Even if it meant she must be tormented forever by the sight of him, the sound of his deep voice, the touch of his hard fingers....

His eyes searched her face, studying her features until she felt her cheeks burning, and a shiver that had nothing to do with the cold air passed through her. "And you?" He pulled her even closer, until the tips of her breasts grazed the creamy wool of his sweater. "Would you miss me if I left now?"

"Yes...for her sake," she said, trying not to feel the heat of his body against hers. She was not dressed to be out here in the snow, and the wind raised goose bumps along her back even while the heat from his chest burned against her. It was like some refined torture, and she wriggled slightly, trying to escape.

The wind had picked up, and it moaned in the pines above them, echoing the small low sound that slipped from her lips as he pressed her closer and let his hands stray around her, pulling golden strings of shivering heat across her back, covered only in a light wool sweater.

"But what about you?" His voice was deep. Hearing it was like looking into a long black well of desire. Dizzied by the vision of that waiting void, she shut her eyes.

"I would survive," she said, hoping for an airy tone but failing, as her lips trembled. His hands were still traveling her back, spinning the golden web that bound her even closer.

"Would you?" His lips were so close now that his breath fell in clean warm waves upon her cheeks. "Would you really?"

Slowly he brushed his mouth against her lips. "You wouldn't miss this?" Her lips parted helplessly, and he ran his tongue like a circle of fire around their soft inner rim. "Or this?"

She shook her head, some small part of her still holding out against him. "No," she whispered.

Her defiance didn't deter him, and he brought his hot hands around to skim her waist, stroke slowly up her rib cage and settle hard against the round flowering of her breast.

"I would..." he murmured against her throat, and her heart pounded in her ears like thunder.

As his hands moved across her breasts, her body churned with need like a sea under a violent storm. Despair took her breath away, as she tried to fight the lapping waves, the breaking crests. Would it always be like this? Would she always tremble at the sight of him and drown in the tidal wave of his lightest touch?

She moaned on an inward gasp. She wouldn't be able to bear it. Oh, she could see why the arrangement appealed to him. He could be near the daughter he loved and have convenient access to the mother he desired. He knew, obviously, that he had only to kiss those well-remembered places, to murmur those well-chosen phrases, and she would melt like ice in the sun. He could take her when it pleased him and forget her when it didn't. He didn't care that he left her aching and bruised, needing the love he didn't feel, craving the tenderness he reserved for others.

She pushed against his head, which was bending ever lower.

"Stop it!" She shivered as he took his head away, leaving her vulnerable to the cruel winter wind. "Leave me alone. I told you—no." She folded her arms across her chest, hoping to hide the revealing swell and thrust that belied her words.

"Let's get this straight once and for all, Drake. I agreed to let you have time with your daughter. I never agreed to be your plaything, as well. You sleep under this roof because you paid for the privilege, but the right to sleep in my bed is not for sale."

He straightened as if she had slapped him, and the bitter look settled over his features again.

"Very well," he said stiffly. "Although I confess to one nagging bit of curiosity."

She raised her brows. "And that is?"

Putting his hands in the pockets of his dark jeans, he shifted his weight casually to one foot. "If I had bought the fur coat for you, instead of for Julie, would your answer be the same?"

At that she did slap him. He didn't flinch or even take his hands from his pockets, but she heard the crack of her palm reverberate in the empty air as she walked away.

CHAPTER TEN

MUCH LATER that night, when everyone else had gone to bed, Amanda tiptoed into the living room, carrying the packages she still needed to wrap. She hadn't accomplished much all day; she'd been too busy contending with her own emotional turmoil and Julie's Christmas Eve jitters. Finally the house was quiet and she could settle down to work.

But in the doorway she stopped, her arms full of foil paper and ribbons and boxes, and stared in dismay, her mouth as dry as sandpaper. Not everyone was safely in bed. Drake was still down here, kneeling in front of a half-assembled bicycle. The room was dim except for the still-lit Christmas tree, a low fire and the desk lamp that shone on the instruction booklet he consulted.

He was so absorbed in his work that he didn't seem to notice her. She told herself to back out quickly while she could and do her wrapping in the kitchen. She couldn't risk another scene. It was Christmas Eve. It should be a time of peace and healing, not bitterness. But her body wouldn't obey, mesmerized by the twinkling white lights from the tree, which threaded his hair with silver and caught like sparks on the wrench he was rapidly twisting.

As always the sight of him left her weak with longing, and one of the packages slipped from her trembling grasp, falling with a clatter to the floor at her feet.

At the sound he looked up from the booklet and leveled his gaze at her. Her heart thumped. Though she had been prepared for a cold reception, she was shocked by what she saw. His blue eyes were absolutely flat, and hard as glass.

"I'm sorry," she apologized idiotically and then wished she could take it back. What in heaven's name was she sorry for? He watched impassively, making no move to help her as she bent to pick up the box.

She fidgeted with it nervously, loath to look at him again. Oddly the dead depths of those flat blue eyes were far more alarming than the anger that had blazed in them at their last meeting. At least anger was human and indicated a living emotion. There was no limit, she thought, to what a man with such cold blue eyes might do.

Her knees began to tremble, and looking up, she placed the clammy palm of her hand on the smooth door frame for support. He wasn't watching her anymore. He had, without a word, simply gone back to his work.

His indifference pinched her pride. Well, he would see that she could feign indifference, too. Head held high, she sailed into the room. Why should she be afraid of him? Why should she be run out of her own living room? It was still her home, and if anyone should leave it should be Drake.

Without speaking she tossed her things down on the coffee table defiantly and then rummaged through the desk drawer, hunting for the Scotch tape.

"Over here." His voice was flat, too, and toneless. Turning, she saw the quick jerk of his head. The tape lay on the floor beside him, along with the clipped ends of wrapping paper he had apparently been using.

"Thanks." She walked swiftly to where the tape lay and picked it up.

For half an hour they sat that way, in total silence, except for the rustle of the gold foil as she wrapped her boxes and the occasional clink of a metal tool against the shining blue chrome of the bicycle. Even the fire was subdued, flickering quietly as it sank farther behind the charred logs.

She couldn't imagine what Drake's thoughts were like, but she knew her own were wretched. Her mind kept reliving the scene with Julie on the hill, kept hearing the angry crack of her hand against his face. How could their love have come to this?

The gold colored paper swam in front of her eyes as she finally faced the truth: there was no hope for them, not now. They had reached the end of their long twisted road. From the moment he had arrived, things had never been simple between them, but today they had gone too far. Today they had said things they couldn't unsay, done things they couldn't forgive.

Amanda rested her head against her hand, letting the scissors dangle uselessly. She could see nothing but heartache ahead. What was left for them? What kind of life would they have, shuttling Julie back and forth between them, sniping at one another over her head?

And how long would it be before Julie sensed the bitterness between her mommy and daddy?

She heard the rippling click of wheels as Drake rolled the finished bicycle toward the tree, but she didn't bother to look up. He would leave now and, though the room would seem even bleaker without him in it, she could at least finish the rest of her work without the disturbing tingle at the small of her back that signaled her awareness of him.

For the moment, though, the tingle grew stronger. She looked up to find him standing over her.

"I guess I'd better get your permission to give Julie the bicycle," he said, still in that nerve-racking monotone. "Are you afraid for her to ride a bike, too?"

She flushed. "No, of course not," she said hotly. "But she doesn't know how to ride a two-wheeler yet. She'll need training wheels."

He inclined his head toward the bike. "They're on."

Still feeling foolish, she looked and nodded. "Oh, yes, I see. That's fine, then."

"So." He raised his dark eyebrows until they disappeared into the fair hair that had fallen onto his forehead. "Do you want a rundown of the other presents? For your official approval, I mean? I wouldn't want to have a scene in the morning in front of Julie."

"Neither would I," she said sharply, "but I'm sure your presents are fine."

Nodding curtly, he turned toward the door. "Good night, then."

He was leaving. Tomorrow they would meet again over the Christmas presents, and smile, and try to keep

Julie from guessing how they really felt. It was a dismal prospect, and her heart was sore with defeat. "Drake..."

"What?" He stopped and gave her his coolly polite attention, but his body was rigid.

She dropped her gaze, hardly knowing what she had meant to say. When he looked at her like that, with his eyes so hard and his body so stiff, she could scarcely believe that their night of love had happened. Could this distant stranger be the same man who had set her soul on fire?

"We can't go on like this," she said impulsively, desperately. "It isn't good for Julie. You can see that, can't you?"

Her desolate tone didn't thaw his frozen expression at all. "Of course I can see that," he said tautly. "What I *can't* see is what we can do about it."

She climbed to her feet, brushing at the green flecks of ribbon that had stuck to her fleecy sweatshirt. "I don't know, either, really." She put her hands on the back of the sofa to steady herself. "I guess I just thought if just once we talked it out...then perhaps we could put it behind us."

He gave a dismissive half turn toward the door, as though disappointed in her words. "I don't think so."

"Oh, I don't mean that we can forgive each other," she said, holding out an imploring hand to stop him. "I know that's not possible. But maybe, for Julie's sake, we could sort it out...and then file it away where it can't hurt her."

His skepticism was visible in the lift of one corner of his wide mouth. "You mean a sort of damage control?"

She nodded, refusing to let his cynicism intimidate her. "I don't care what you call it. I mean, work out some kind of understanding so that we can coexist peaceably. I have some suggestions, and I'm sure you do, too...."

He shrugged and came back into the room. "All right," he said indifferently. "Why not?"

Relief flooded her, and she sat on the couch, though he remained standing, his arms crossed in front of his broad chest in an attitude of repressed hostility.

His brows up inquiringly, he spoke in measured tones, implying a patience his tight body silently contradicted. "You said you had some suggestions."

She swallowed hard, wishing suddenly that she could run away. But there was nowhere to run anymore. Fate seemed to have locked them in a cage together, and they had to find a way to make peace, or destroy one another forever.

"All right." She lifted her chin as she spoke. "Well, first of all I think it would be better if you didn't—didn't touch me, at least not the way you did today. It makes me...uncomfortable, and I think it would upset Julie."

His lip curled, showing a flash of white teeth. "Upset our daughter to see her parents kissing?"

She blushed. "You know what I mean. Given the way things are... Well, we're not the same as other parents, Drake."

"That's an understatement." He let his gaze slide over her body. "But if that's what you want, you've got it. I won't—" his eyes came back up to her face "—touch you anymore. You have my word."

She shifted uneasily on the nubby fabric. A wave of emptiness had swept through her as he made his promise. But it was for the best, she assured herself. It was for the best.

"Thank you," she said awkwardly and rubbed her hand across the hard seam of the upholstered seat. "I think that will help." She looked up at him. "And what about you? Is there anything I can do that would help make things easier for you?"

He laughed, a brittle sound that had no mirth in it, and moved toward the French doors. The small panes of glass split the snowy view beyond into a dozen swirling scenes.

"Yes . . . you could stop looking so damn desirable. That might help."

Looking at his back, she clenched her hands in her lap, unable to tell whether he was serious or not. How could she answer such a statement?

"I fight that battle, too, you know," she said, surprising herself with her candor. An hour ago such an admission would have been unthinkable, like alerting the enemy to a weak spot in your defenses. But she finally understood that only honesty would suffice in a moment as dire as this. There was no room for false pride in the prison they had created for themselves.

He didn't turn around, his dark body silhouetted in black against the blue velvet sky. "Yes," he said heavily, "I do know. That's what makes it so impossible, isn't it? If it weren't for that we could be just another set of amicably divorced parents. Just another sad statistic."

She looked at her hands, mutely acknowledging the truth of what he said. Julie could survive having divorced parents. Children all over the world managed to grow up, more or less emotionally intact, in broken homes. But what Julie could *not* endure were the vicious currents of hostility and desire that met and formed such a dangerous whirlpool around her. No child should have to watch love drown slowly, painfully, in that churning sea.

She shifted her weight on the sofa, rubbing absently at her leg, which was aching slightly. She was always more aware of it during periods of stress.

"Maybe with time," she ventured, "it will get easier, if we don't see each other as much. Maybe living under the same roof has—"

He jerked around, the tree's lights revealing an angrily twitching muscle in his jaw. "Do you really believe that, Amanda? We've spent six years without so much as seeing each other's face, and look at us! How many years will it take?"

She slipped her hand under her right knee nervously, absently fingering the thin jagged scar. She knew he was right, but what other hope was there? What did he want to do about it? As long as they were sharing custody of Julie . . . Her heart stopped briefly as she considered the possibility that he might no longer want to share Julie. Was it possible he was going to offer to bow out now? Or—and at the thought her heart picked up with a crazy beat—was he going to ask *her* to give Julie up to him?

As her frantic eyes darted to his she realized he was staring at her leg. Slowly she pulled her hand free and smoothed the blue sweatpants over her knee. Why had she taunted him that first day with that foolish lie about the Alps? She mustn't antagonize him by re-minding him of it now.

But it was too late. His dark eyes were fixed on her leg still, and they were narrowing thoughtfully.

"I want you to tell me something," he said in a low voice.

She looked up at him helplessly, the blood beating in her cheeks like tiny frightened wings. "What?"

"Tell me why you're afraid of that hill."

Her lips parted. "I...I was just afraid she'd get hurt. It's dangerous."

"No, it's not." His voice was coiled so tightly she almost didn't recognize it. "Webster and I were being very careful. And someone has put a fence there, down at the bottom, before the street. She wasn't in any danger at all, and yet you were terrified. It wasn't a normal reaction, Mandy. What is it that frightens you?"

Her mind raced like a rat in a maze looking for a way out. But there was none. At every turn she ran up against the dead end of the truth.

Summoning her courage, she stood up and faced him. "I was hurt there," she said slowly. "I fell down that hill." She looked at him, marveling at how sim-ple the truth sounded. "That's how I hurt my leg. There was a car coming, and I fell into its path."

His lips were thin lines. "Fell? Or ran?"

Her brows knit. Did he already know? Shame stained her cheeks. Perhaps he'd always known. Per-haps he had seen her in his rearview mirror as she'd stumbled after him that night, and had chosen to ig-nore her. "Ran," she murmured. "I was running."

"I thought so."

His eyes flicked hard across her face and then down again to her right leg. Under his dark gaze she felt suddenly as though the leg would buckle. Her face flamed as, against her will, she remembered how his hands had stroked across the curving scar, accepting it with the same loving devotion he had given the rest of her body. Now his eyes were so black and angry that their perusal was like an insult.

"Was the idea of having my child so repugnant to you?" His voice was brittle. "Or was it just that you couldn't face your grandmother? Didn't you know there are easier ways to get rid of unwanted babies? Surely your good doctor could have arranged something."

Amanda shook her head, trying to understand. His words were spoken with such bitterness. How could he think—

"Are you mad? What are you talking about?" She squinted and blinked as tears blinded her eyes again. "Do you think I was trying to...to *hurt* myself?"

"Perhaps. Or perhaps you were just trying to—" he swallowed, too "—free yourself of me. Of my child."

She gripped the sofa so hard the fabric burned her fingertips. At first a baffled fury froze her tongue, and then words were spilling out like lava from an erupting volcano.

She moved toward him blindly, her hands clenched. As hot tears rained from her eyes, scalding her cheeks, she lost what little control she had left and beat her fists against his hard chest. "Damn you, Drake! You never knew me at all, did you? All you saw was a spoiled little rich girl. You never knew I had grown up, that I was ready to be your wife. That I was ready to have your child and follow you anywhere in the world."

He imprisoned her flailing fists in his own strong hands. "Shh," he murmured, as she choked on her angry tears. "Shh, Mandy. Be still."

She writhed in his grasp. "No!" She looked up at him through wetly burning eyes. "I guess I didn't know you very well, either, Drake. I thought you were the most wonderful man I'd ever met. I thought you were worth running after, worth throwing everything away for, worth chasing down that godforsaken hill." She dragged in a torn breath and, finally stilling her punishing hands, dropped her head hopelessly onto them. "I thought you loved me."

His grip on her hands tightened, and he spoke slowly, as though not totally in control of his vocal chords. "Amanda, I don't think I understand. Tell me carefully—and try to be calm. When did you fall? When were you chasing me?"

It was no struggle to be calm. She was utterly drained from her emotional outburst, and she spoke quietly into her hands. "The night you left Mount Larkin. The night my grandmother paid you to leave me."

She felt the deep expansion of his chest as he pulled in a disbelieving breath. "You were there that night?"

She nodded numbly, not looking up. "Of course I was."

"She told me you were out—with your fiancé...." He was silent a long tense moment. "But—if you were there—then why did you have to chase me? If you wanted to see me, why didn't you just come in while I was talking to Olivia?"

Anger shot through her, reviving her, and she yanked out of his grasp. What kind of ridiculous question was that? Was this still a game to him? Didn't he see yet what he and Olivia had done to her, and to Julie? The bitterness she had held back all these years boiled over again.

"Because I wasn't supposed to know you were there, was I? You came in the darkness with your blackmail, and you and Olivia were deliberately circumspect during the negotiations. No raised voices. All very civilized."

His eyes flickered, as though in response to an inner pain. Perhaps it pricked his ego to have his perfidy laid out in plain English. She balled her fists at her sides and let her bitterness have free rein.

"I didn't have the *pleasure* of hearing any of it, but she told me later how it all went. I can just see it. You were always good at imitations, Drake. I'll bet you did a terrific imitation of a sleazy cowhand. Did you hold your hat in your hands and speak very politely? 'You want your granddaughter to marry a rich fella, don't you, ma'am? Well, it'll be pretty tough to land one of them if word gets out that she's been sleeping with the gardener. I'd love to take a long trip back home to Texas, but I just can't afford it, ma'am.' And she just couldn't wait to pull out her checkbook, could she?"

She bit her lower lip and breathed through her nose, her nostrils flaring. "And I never would have known anything about it if I hadn't heard your car pulling away. Remember that car, Drake?" She shot her words out venomously. "It wasn't sleek and powerful like the Jaguar, was it? It rumbled and roared—and it gave you away!"

"Gave me away?" Finally a reaction. His dark eyebrows contracted over his hard blue eyes, and he reached out to grab her forearm. Quickly she twisted clear of his grip. She didn't want him to touch her now. Not ever again. "Is that really what you think happened that night? You think I *asked* for that money? Are you telling me you didn't know I was coming? You didn't tell Olivia to get rid of me for you?"

Her lips curled. "Tell her to? I was desperately in love with you. I thought I was pregnant with your child. You think I asked her to get rid of you?"

She began to laugh, a sharp glassy sound that splintered the air around them. "No, Drake. Unless you think I'm a mental case, you're going to have to come up with a scenario that makes more sense than that!"

He frowned, and what appeared to be stunned confusion slowed his words. "But Olivia told me that you were going to marry another man, a rich man, and that's exactly what you did. A doctor, one of 'your kind.'"

She almost laughed again, but the irony was too bitter. "Richard was no rich man, Drake. He was the kind of doctor who hardly ever sent out a bill—he said sick people shouldn't be hounded. He lived in the country, real redneck Georgia country, most of his life. He had just come to Atlanta a couple of years before he met me. And he only came then because he was sick and needed a good neurologist."

Drake shook his head, as though trying to shake the thoughts into place. "Why, then? Why?"

"Because he cared, that's why!" She felt the tears again, and she spoke harshly, trying to push them back. "He was in the emergency room that night, and he took care of me after the accident. He stood by when I told Olivia I wouldn't get rid of the baby. We needed each other. He needed a friend, someone to help him through his illness. And I needed a friend, too. I also needed a place to live, since Olivia had told me that 'the Daniels bastard' would not be welcome at Mount Larkin. And I needed a name for the baby, since you clearly had no intention of giving it your own."

She heard the anger settle into her voice, turning it as hard and cold as the winter ground outside. "You thought all this time that I was just a fortune hunter? You'd better think again, Drake. I doubt that even the toughest gold digger would trade in a sexy young writer for the chance to get disinherited, bear an illegitimate baby and marry a forty-eight-year-old country doctor who was dying."

Drake ran his long fingers through his golden hair, brushing it away from his furrowed brow. "I..." He seemed at a loss for words, his deep voice husky. He rubbed his eyes, as though pressing back the threat of tears. When he spoke again, a primitive emotion had altered his voice. "Mandy..."

Still frozen she didn't answer. He stared a long moment, his eyes unreadable, focused just over her head.

"You really didn't know, did you?" Finally he spoke—softly, as though talking only to his memories, as though she was not even in the room. "You didn't know. She was lying...."

Amanda stared out at the snow dumbly, neither inviting him to continue nor stopping him. Her misery and anger were like suffocating gasses, strangling any sound at all.

"She said you'd told her all about our affair," he said, his voice dull. "She said you had decided you'd made a mistake. You wanted to marry another man, a man who was 'one of your own kind.' Those were her exact words. But you were worried, she said, that I might crop up at an inconvenient moment and embarrass you. So for your sake she was willing to pay me to go back to Texas."

Amanda was glad he couldn't see her face. She felt her eyes squint at the words, registering both horror and disbelief. And yet... and yet it did have the ring of truth—it sounded just like Olivia....

"And you believed her?"

"Yes," he answered slowly. "I believed her. She asked me to think of your welfare, said you 'regretted your indiscretion' and hoped it wouldn't wreck your future. God how I hated you that night."

The anguish in his words touched a chord within her, and she felt helpless tears prick at her eyes. She turned around, and the sight of his stiff misery twisted at her heart.

"But why, Drake? Why believe her without even asking me? Hadn't I told you, in every way a woman can tell a man, how much I loved you?"

He jammed his fists in his pockets. "I guess I had always thought it was too good to be true. You were a Larkin, with everything that came with the name." He waved his hand at the Georgian columns visible outside the window, and the stately pines that dotted the grounds. "And I was a nobody from a little Texas town. I had nothing to offer you. I'd been half waiting for you to come to your senses all along."

She murmured a small groan of protest, but he kept talking. "I didn't see how else she could have known about us—we'd been so careful. You were so young, Mandy, and so afraid of someone finding out and telling her. Remember how you said she could ruin anything, even our love? You were so afraid...." He shook his head slowly. "And so, like a fool, I humored you. I made sure we weren't seen, and I never told anyone about us. When she knew, I figured you had to have been the one who told her."

Amanda laughed mirthlessly. "It was Cicely," she said bitterly. "I had confided in her just that afternoon. I was ready to make a decision—either to tell Olivia or to pack my things and run away to you. I didn't tell Cicely that I thought I might be pregnant. I just told her I loved you. She promised she wouldn't betray me." She laughed again. "But of course, she did. For my own good, she said later."

He let out a long low breath. "My god—It was Cicely. I would never have guessed Cicely."

She smiled thinly. "I know. Trusting her, when she was so susceptible to Olivia's influence, was an incredibly ill-advised move. But as you said, I was so young. That's only one of many mistakes I wouldn't make today."

Unable to meet the desolation she saw in his eyes, she turned away. She couldn't seem to sort it all out. Could that really be how it had happened? Could Olivia have told one lie to her, another to Drake?

Could such lies really have wrecked the lives of three people?

The turbulence around her heart seemed to rise up and choke her. The room felt too hot, too close, and impulsively she pulled open the doors, revealing the hushed and peaceful scene beyond. The night was beautiful, a Christmas-card night. The frantic scramble of snowflakes had finally ceased, and the sky was like a swath of spangled blue velvet stretched above the pure white of the earth.

She walked a few feet out onto the white-draped patio, and she heard the soft crunch of snow as he followed her. He stood very still beside her at the balustrade, and the light wind feathered his hair away from his brow. He looked young right now, as well—young and vulnerable.

His voice was low. "Am I one of the mistakes you're too wise to make again?"

She didn't answer immediately. As always when she was in his presence, her body was too intensely aware of him to allow clear thought. Her heart was pounding in her throat, and a heat that she could no longer ignore was building in her abdomen. She looked away from his earnest face into the blank expanse of snow beyond, hoping to turn down the flame. "I don't know," she said finally. "I don't know what to do."

He looked straight ahead. When he spoke, his low monotone sounded almost indifferent, as though the details didn't matter anymore. "I tore it up, you know. Her money, like her snobbery and her cruelty, made me sick, and I told her so."

Amanda breathed deeply, drinking in the clean silence, and looked up through the bare branches of an aged oak, branches that seemed to jigsaw the full moon. The air was fresh, as if the snow had sponged away all impurities from it.

Somewhere from far away the echoing bark of a dog carried in the still air, but otherwise everything was profoundly quiet. Not the smallest wind whispered through the pines. They were alone with the echoes of the past. Just an old woman's lies—all these years, all this heartache. All lies.

She wrapped her hands around her upper arms and bowed her head as she spoke. "I wasn't afraid of anything when I was with you. I was only afraid to go without your love," she whispered, as her numbness evaporated and tears pricked at her eyes. "I was afraid you'd just wanted the money, that it had all been an act when you were with me."

"An act?" Finally he smiled, and the warmth of that familiar smile reached deep inside her, as though stirring at the settled smoldering embers. "Dear god! You turned me inside out, Mandy. No one could have pretended that."

His voice was low, and it sent a feather of anticipation down her spine. He stood just inches in front of her, but she didn't move, didn't encourage him to close those last inches.

He stared at her a long moment and then looked away, toward the western slope of the property. The moonlight slid down the hill, fading to darkness halfway down, and the effect made the slope seem even steeper than it was. She followed his gaze and shuddered involuntarily.

"Don't, Drake," she called, knowing instinctively that he was imagining her reckless flight down the hill.

His face, in profile, was brooding as he surveyed the slope, and then he turned around, as though measuring the distance from house to street. His mouth was a tight line.

"Dammit, Mandy." His voice was raw. "It was insane. It's too far, and I was driving too fast. You couldn't possibly have caught me."

She nodded, pressing her fists against her stomach to quell the panic that churned there whenever she looked at the hill, whenever she *really* looked at it and remembered. "I know," she said softly. "But I had to try."

Suddenly he pressed both hands over his face, smothering a curse. He stood that way for a long moment, and then roughly he reached out and pressed his palms against the balustrade, on either side of her body, so close she could smell the soft wool of his sweater but not close enough to touch her.

"Forget what she told you," he said raspingly. "Forget it all, do you hear?" He still didn't hold her, but he let his forehead rest against hers, and she could feel his breath misting against her lips. "She can't hurt us anymore. It's all over."

She shut her eyes as he kissed her cold cheek, his lips like hot ice.

His voice was deep with conviction, and something else, something hungry. "I love you. I always have— and I *know* you love me. So say you'll marry me, Mandy. You can make the past six years disappear with just one word." She felt the balustrade shudder as his arms tensed with the effort to restrain his need. "Say it—say yes and let me hold you."

Her throat was too tight to allow words to pass. Silently, but with a feeling of coming home, she simply rested her head against his broad chest.

His arms came violently around her, and he buried his hot lips in her cool hair, murmuring soft phrases against it. And there, finally in the safety of his arms, she opened the dam she had erected years ago and allowed the waves of emotion to sweep through her, crashing into one another as she listened to the steady rhythm of Drake's heart against her ear. For the first time in her life she saw clearly how pathetic Olivia had been—and she felt free. . . .

"Hey, come back here." Drake's voice broke into her thoughts as he cupped her chin in his hands, tilting her face toward his. "This is no time for daydreaming. I said, you are going to marry me."

"Oh, yes . . ." she breathed, joy brimming in her voice as she threw her arms around his broad shoulders. "Yes, I'm going to marry you." She could feel his heart throbbing harder now against her breast. "If your daughter doesn't mind, that is."

"She won't," he said, grinning wickedly and running his hands hungrily through her hair. "She likes me—we're going to write books together, and we just may let *you* do the pictures." He nibbled at her ear, and his lips were electric against her chilled skin. "Besides," he whispered, "she told Webster she thinks I'm pretty."

"Don't be vain about it," Amanda murmured, a ripple of laughter in her voice. "She just likes your eyes. . . ."

But her voice trailed off as desire zigzagged like lightning from his lips down into the very core of her.

She pressed her body closer to his, and she reached to pull his sweater free of his belt.

His muscles clenched as her cold fingers slipped under the sweater and met the hot rippled wall of his chest. His grip tightened possessively, and he looked down at her. Then she trembled, too, at the power of the naked love that had mated with open desire in his handsome face.

"Drake—" she ran her hands up the hard swell of his chest. "Drake, I love you."

"Do you, my darling?" He smiled raggedly. "Then we'd better tell Julie that her daddy has come home for Christmas."

She laughed, and brushed her lips against the pulse that raced in his throat. "I don't know.... She wanted a puppy."

"We'll get her that, too." He laughed and buried his face in her hair, breathing deeply, as though to fill himself with the smell of her. "And for next Christmas—maybe a baby brother?"

He held her away from him, just far enough to look into her face. He ran gentle fingers over her brow, tracing her wide, tear-moistened eyes. "Yes, a brother, I think. A baby boy with laughing green eyes, and his mother's beautiful hair...."

She tried to offer a teasing response, but words wouldn't come. He must have read her brimming eyes, for he smiled into them with a look so tender that her own tremulous smile shook and then disappeared as his lips closed over hers.

Under that fervent touch, the past dissolved like melting snow, and the future began at last.

Coming Next Month

1191 NO WAY TO SAY GOODBYE Kay Gregory
Gareth Mardon closes his Vancouver office and heartlessly dismisses the staff.
Roxane Peters is furious—and she has no compunctions about making her
feelings quite clear to Gareth. Only somehow, it seems, her feelings are
threatened, too....

1192 THE HEAT IS ON Sarah Holland
When Steve Kennedy erupts into Lorel's life, she has the very uncomfortable
feeling she's met him before. Yet it's impossible to ignore him, for he proves to
be the screenwriter on the film in which she wants the leading role.

1193 POTENTIAL DANGER Penny Jordan
Young Kate had been too passionately in love to care about the future. Now a
mature woman, Kate has learned to take care of herself and her daughter. But
no matter how she tries she can't stop loving Silas Edwards, the man who
betrayed her.

1194 DEAL WITH THE DEVIL Sandra Marton
Elena marries Blake Rogan to get out of her revolution-torn country on an
American passport. She believes Rogan married her in a deal with her father
for hard cash. But Rogan just wants to get out alive—with or without Elena.

1195 SWEET CAPTIVITY Kate Proctor
Kidnapped and imprisoned along with famous film director Pascal de
Perregaux, Jackie is prey to all sorts of feelings. Most disturbing is her
desperate attraction to Cal, her fellow victim—especially since he believes she
is in league with their abductors....

1196 CHASE THE DAWN Kate Walker
Desperate for money to restore her little sister's health, Laurel approaches her
identical twin sister's estranged husband. She's forgotten just how much like
her twin she looks—and she finds herself impersonating her sister and
"married" to the formidable Hal Rochester.

1197 DRIVING FORCE Sally Wentworth
Maddy's divorce from racing-car driver West Marriott was painful. He is no
longer part of her life. Now West needs her professional help after an accident.
Maddy isn't sure, though, that she can treat her ex-husband as just
another client!

1198 WHEN THE GODS CHOOSE Patricia Wilson
Arrogant Jaime Carreras is the most insulting man Sara has ever met. Why
should she care what he thinks of her? Unfortunately, however, Jaime is the
only man who can help her trace her father in the wilds of Mexico.

Available in August wherever paperback books are sold, or through
Harlequin Reader Service:

In the U.S.
901 Fuhrmann Blvd.
P.O. Box 1397
Buffalo, N.Y. 14240-1397

In Canada
P.O. Box 603
Fort Erie, Ontario
L2A 5X3

Harlequin Regency Romance™

Romance the way it was *always* meant to be!

The time is 1811, when a Regent Prince rules the empire. The place is London, the glittering capital where rakish dukes and dazzling debutantes scheme and flirt in a dangerously exciting game. Where marriage is the passport to wealth and power, yet every girl hopes secretly for love....

Welcome to Harlequin Regency Romance where reading is an adventure and romance is *not* just a thing of the past! Two delightful books a month.

Available wherever Harlequin Books are sold.